CIRCLE OF LIGHT

A PERSIMMON HOLLOW CHRISTMAS NOVELLA

PERSIMMON HOLLOW LEGACY SERIES

GERRI BAUER

SPIRANTHES PRESS, LLC, DELAND, FLORIDA

Circle of Light
A Persimmon Hollow Christmas Novella

This is a work of fiction. Names, characters, corporations, institutions, organizations, events, or locales in this novel are either the product of the author's imagination or, if real, used fictitiously. The resemblance of any character to any actual persons (living or dead) is entirely coincidental.

Editor: Ericka McIntyre, https://www.erickamcintyre.com/

Cover art: SelfPubBookCovers.com/ RLSather

ISBN
979-8-9866600-7-3 (digital)
979-8-9866600-8-0 (general paperback)
979-8-9866600-5-9 (Amazon paperback)
979-8-9866600-4-2 (Kindle)
Copyright ©2023, Gerri Bauer
All rights reserved

Published by Spiranthes Press, LLC
DeLand, Florida, USA

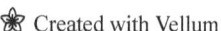 Created with Vellum

To my husband, Peter D. Bauer,
and in beloved memory of both my and his parents:
Catherine Rose Puccio Giovanelli
Edward Michael Giovanelli
Joanne Bronson Bauer
Harold Eason Bauer Jr.

PART I

November 27, 1898

Advent, Week One—Hope

Clara DeForest looked at the calendar atop the rolltop desk. Again. As though the weather outdoors would heed her glance and snap to attention.

In a few days it would be December 1. Advent, December, and the Christmas season meant snow or at least cold temperatures. Mugs of cocoa by the fireside. Watching friends ice skate. Mittens, hats, and scarves; chilly rides in a sleigh. Not this half-autumn, half-summer oddness.

Thanksgiving had been strange enough. They had dined outdoors in eighty-five-degree weather. A handful of days later, Advent began on the earliest possible date for the season's start. It had been another eighty-degree day.

God, are you reminding me where I am? she asked silently. *Believe me, I'm aware.*

She could only imagine what Christmas Eve and Christmas Day would be like in weather that resembled summer.

"You're making yourself miserable," said her sister, Meg, as she walked into the parlor. She held a bright orange globe-shaped tangerine in each hand. "Your sigh was loud enough to carry halfway across town."

"I didn't sigh," said Clara. Truly, she hadn't. Had she?

"See what I mean," said Meg. "Here, take one. I brought one for each of us. Let's eat them outside. They're juicy and Mama wouldn't be pleased to find citrus stains on the sofa."

Clara followed her sister out to the porch. It was easy for Meg to be cheery. Her beau, Harvey, had joined the family's exodus to this wilderness of heat, junglelike woods, glaring sunshine, and paths of sugary sand instead of snow. There hadn't even been an apple harvest in what was supposed to be autumn. Apples didn't grow here. Nor did sugar maples. The trees around her still retained their leaves.

The region's tangled green growth was broken by rows of neat, rounded citrus trees and clusters of pine forests that towered over settlements. She'd been astonished at the forbidding wildernesses that stretched for miles around every town they'd passed through on their journey to Persimmon Hollow. Her incredulity about the family's new home grew when the weather hardly changed from day to day to day. Nothing indicated summer had ended. Days stretched into circles of sunshine, occasional bursts of fierce rains, and sticky heat.

Now the most hopeful season of the year had arrived, and it resembled nothing more than another day of sameness.

"Yum," said Meg, after she peeled her tangerine, pulled off a section and ate it. "C'mon, cheer up, Clara. It's not that bad here."

"For you, maybe," said Clara. She pouted, leaned on the porch railing and tried to ignore the tangy-sweet scent of citrus. Her mouth started to water. She pressed her lips together. She wouldn't eat any of the tangerine. That would be giving in to the enemy—citrus fever—that had lured her father here.

"You have Harvey and a wedding to plan. I have nothing."

"Except me and Harvey, and our brother, our parents and all the people here who've been so welcoming, and—"

"Oh, you know what I mean," said Clara, with a weary wave of her hand.

Meg stopped snacking and studied Clara. "You're acting like a two-year-old instead of a twenty-two-year-old."

"If I were two I wouldn't be thinking about the lack of available men here. Not that I'm looking, mind you. I've accepted my state in life. No one would want me anyway."

"Oh, Clara! There's a special man for you, somewhere. Maybe here! There's a single man every time you turn around. I've never seen so many unattached men, especially some of the homesteaders putting in their groves and tending new farms."

"I mean *suitable* men," Clara objected. Although she too had noticed some of the homesteaders. She had no idea whether any were suitable, or even what suitable looked like for someone like her. They all dressed alike and looked vaguely similar when working on their groves and farms.

"A hard-working homesteader needs a strong, active woman, not an invalid like me," she added. Someone who can bear children, her internal voice whispered.

"There's a fair number of young people in town and lots of things you can do," said Meg, ignoring Clara's comment about being an invalid.

"I heard there's a literary society and a thespian group," Meg said. "We're just steps from the heart of town. You can walk that far without trouble. Papa was so lucky to get this property and business opportunity. It's his dream come true. Look how excited Melvin is about helping him. I've never seen our brother so happy. Harvey, too. He's already building extra furniture for store inventory."

3

"What about Mother?" Clara pointed out. "She wasn't especially happy about moving here." Clara hadn't been the only one unenthusiastic about exchanging northern city life for a small Florida citrus grove and downtown furniture store.

"True," said Meg, and smacked her lips. She'd gone back to savoring the citrus. For some reason, Meg's cheerfulness soured Clara's mood even more.

"In case you didn't notice, Mama is much happier lately," Meg said. "Ever since she joined the Altar Society and the new Benevolent Society for the Orphaned and Needy. You don't see her moping around the house."

Clara didn't want to hear another word. "It's so hot out here," she said. "There's no breeze. The sun is too bright. It'll probably bleach the color from my eyes and they're pale enough already. Even my hair is sweating, I'm convinced."

She undid her loose bun, untangled and retwisted her waist-long light-brown hair and pinned it up again. "I'm going in, Meg, and drawing the drapes tight against the sun," she said. Fanning herself, she walked toward the door, her heels clicking with determination against the floorboards.

"I'll pray for you, that you don't wallow in self-pity much longer," Meg called as the screen door squeaked when Clara pulled it open. Clara didn't answer, just clomped inside the house.

"Gosh, this tangerine is good," Meg said aloud as she finished the last piece. "Try giving thanks for what you have instead of pining after what you think you want, Clara," she said in a low voice to the now-closed door.

❧

Clara worked on her embroidery until her head ached. Only a few more feather stitches and she'd be at a good stopping point. The bits of thread looked vaguely like chicken feet and reminded her of footsteps. The steps she would take to travel back north permanently if she had her own income. Okay, yes, if she had Mama and Papa's approval, too. She knew they'd never give it. Not to the family weakling, always fawned over for her frailness and delicate health.

She gave thanks they'd at least granted permission for her to travel north for her friend Beth's wedding at the end of December. She was one of the attendants. How could she not go? It would be a quick trip, there and back in little over a week so she'd be home in time for Epiphany. Her parents had insisted on that.

Maybe, just maybe, they'd let her return north permanently if she lived with a relative. Maybe Aunt Hattie. She was already staying with her for the wedding. Clara was certain her eccentric but loving aunt would be amenable to a long-term arrangement.

Why hadn't she thought of that before? She'd write to Aunt Hattie right away. Right now, so she'd receive the letter before Clara arrived for the wedding. That way the conversation could start before she actually returned north.

Clara stood up and stretched and flexed her wrists and fingers while she considered what she'd pen when she got upstairs to her room.

The family's home fronted the main boulevard that went through the heart of Persimmon Hollow. Something was happening just outside the house. Clara pulled open the drapes enough to peek out. A flash of sunlight poured through the gap in the cotton damask. The sun seemed to mock her for sitting in a dim room instead of stitching outside in the brightness and fresh air.

No, she thought. She wouldn't let the sun win any more than she'd let citrus win. She'd rather see white snowflakes falling on a muffled landscape. Even if snow did make her fingers and toes blue with cold.

The noise outside turned out to be nothing more than her

brother, Melvin, and a couple of store employees untying, unwrapping, and removing a grandfather clock from its secure perch in the back of a wagon. She knew the clock's final destination, the corner of the parlor. She picked up her needlework and headed upstairs so she'd be out of their way.

She passed her mother on the stairs.

"Clara!" said Gertrude DeForest. "I was just looking for you. Do you wish to join the Altar Society?"

Clara hesitated, unwilling to admit she didn't. It was something for the older women. Plus it might make everyone think she was willing to put down roots in Persimmon Hollow.

Her mother knew her too well. "Yes, I know there are few women your age there. But," she placed her hand on Clara's arm, "surely you'd do us a generous favor and embroider a chasuble for Father O'Connell. You don't have to join the society to do that. We'd like to gift him the chasuble for Gaudete Sunday."

Clara gaped at her.

"You want me to embroider a chasuble in two weeks? Less than two weeks, even! Mother, that's not a lot of time. Plus, I have to get ready for my trip—you know, prepare my clothes and pack and all."

"I know, time is a factor. That's why we decided on a simple but elegant design. Come, let me show you. You'll see that it's doable. Meg and I are prepared to help if needed. All you have to do is ask."

Mother's suggestions were usually commands. Clara followed her mother, who'd turned around and went back up the stairs and into the master bedroom.

"Isn't this beautiful?" Gertrude asked after she drew a paper from her dressing table drawer, unfolded it, and showed a sketch to Clara. "See how the design will fit nicely on the center of the fabric: a large cross with the letters IHS in a circle at the center, plus a few grape leaves, a small cluster of grapes, and two sheaths of wheat, one on each side. Simple but elegant."

Clara's gloom lifted despite her determination to stay in a mood, her only form of protest for her current life situation.

"Yes, I thought you'd approve," her mother said. "You can see how we penciled in our preferred thread colors. So, what do you think?"

For the first time since arriving in Persimmon Hollow six months earlier, Clara felt a shimmer of hope. If nothing else, the project would keep her busy. Plus, it would allow her to decline social events. The first handful had given her all the taste she needed of Persimmon Hollow society.

Yes, everyone was welcoming and friendly. But she wasn't the feisty pioneer type so many local women seemed to be. She didn't know what to say when they started talking about citrus harvests, canning sessions, wild hogs rooting in flower beds, and cows blocking the railroad tracks.

She also knew better than to decline a request from her mother.

"I'd be happy to," she said.

"Good," said Gertrude. She returned the design paper to the dresser drawer and organized the other contents around it. "I've gotten word that the town dressmaker has finished sewing the chasuble. You can go pick it up at her shop and select the thread while you're there."

Clara's sliver of hope faded at the thought. She walked over to the window and looked out, toward the heart of Persimmon Hollow. "Town" was so unlike what she had known in the city. Some of the storefronts looked like pictures she'd seen of Wild West gold rush towns, right down to the wooden sidewalks.

The people were different, too. Their likes and behaviors were nothing like those of the company she was used to keeping. They seemed to have little use for the skills she'd mastered at the Gentle Ladies Arts Academy back home, things like deportment and elocution and comportment and posture and drawing and French. Although, in truth, she'd been better at organizing language books and arranging art prints for display than she'd been at conversing in French or reciting poetry. Her organizational skills had even drawn the attention of the principal, who had recommended her to the local historical society for a museum project.

Oh, how she missed her museum project. She'd been surprised when the historical society asked her to develop plans for a small facility and exhibit focused on local history. The hours she spent in their archives had set her imagination awhirl. She'd been immersed in ideas when the family's move to Florida had shaken her world. No one had told her until everything was decided. They hadn't wanted to upset her delicate constitution, her parents said.

Clara squeezed her eyes shut for a moment. She thought again about her student days. Life had seemed so easy.

She wondered if the refinement arts were even taught at the DeLand Academy and College everyone here seemed to prize. She doubted it. She'd heard it emphasized academics.

But even Clara realized she couldn't hide forever in the house, one of the few things she liked about Persimmon Hollow. The family's two-story Victorian-style house with its turret room and wraparound porch reminded her of home. Her old home.

She turned around and saw her mother had finished her task and stood waiting, watching Clara with a soft gaze full of warmth and love.

"Remember that it's Advent, dear," Gertrude said. "The season of hope."

Clara stepped into the open doorway to the dressmaker's shop on Persimmon Boulevard and halted when she saw another customer there. She stopped and took a minute to collect herself. She was flushed from heat and fatigue after the three-block walk.

She used to enjoy taking slow walks around the city's streets back home. Her shortness of breath today must be due to the warmth and humidity. Three blocks had always been possible before. Well, most of the time.

"I don't know what color, Josefa." A tall blond man stood at the counter, hands pressed down upon it, and frowned at the array of thread a dark-haired woman had set before him. "I don't even know why they sent me to pick this up. I'm a man of many talents but needlework ain't one of them."

He laughed and the woman did, too. "Oh, everybody knows that," she said. "If Aunt Lupita has complained once about how hard you are on your clothing, she's complained a hundred times. Always with a smile on her face, too, as she mends the holes in the fabric. And you old enough to mend your own jeans."

"I love your Aunt Lupita," the young man said. "I wish she were here right now to tell me if she and my mother really said they want stuff called crewel thread or something else. But soon as they heard I was headed into town to pick up my new saddle, they saddled me with this extra chore."

He guffawed at his play on words. The young woman also giggled. Clara, too, felt her lips curve at the guy's silly comment.

Out of habit, she closed the door behind her when she took a full step inside. A small bell on a string above the door jingled.

The young man and woman looked up, startled.

"Oh, hello!" the young woman said. "Please come in. I didn't hear you enter. I had the door open to catch a breeze. It's unseasonably warm this year."

The young man stared at Clara and seemed momentarily stunned. She, too, felt a little jolt. He was so handsome and robust. He reminded her of health and sturdiness and everything good about the outdoors.

"Hey! Hello!" the young man said, recovering and striding toward her with arm outstretched. "May I introduce myself? Bill Taylor, at your service. And you are—?"

Gosh, he was forward, Clara thought, and took an involuntary step back. Young men usually waited for a mutual acquaintance to introduce them. Was she supposed to shake his hand? Was there any social protocol in Persimmon Hollow?

"Think of him as a friendly puppy who doesn't always recognize boundaries," the young woman said as she followed Billy and nudged his hand away from Clara. "I'm Josefa Gomez Rodriguez Stillman, owner of the shop," she said to Clara. "He is, as he said, Bill Taylor of Taylor Grove, a couple of miles out from town."

Read Josefa's story in Stitching A Life in Persimmon Hollow
(Persimmon Hollow Legacy Series, Book 2)

Clara had heard of Taylor Grove, the heart of the local Catholic community. There was even an orphanage on the large property, run by Sisters of St. Francis. She wondered if this Bill fellow was related to the owner of the grove.

"How can I help you?" Josefa asked. "You're new here, aren't you? I've seen you at Mass. Welcome!"

Clara responded with a nod and quiet smile, introduced herself, and explained her quest as the three moved back toward the counter. Josefa twirled and disappeared into a curtained-off room, calling over her shoulder as she walked through a break in the fabric. "The chasuble is in here, it'll only take me a minute to get it. Wait until you see it! The silk fabric has such a nice drape."

Bill shifted from foot to foot and continued to look alternately at Clara and the thread.

"Maybe you can help me?" he asked, and ran a hand through his hair. "What's the difference between this stuff?"

Clara took a step closer to the counter. She was overly aware of his presence beside her. He certainly had a nice look about him. Fit and strong and looking as though he'd just taken a break from outdoor work. Of course, she thought. That's exactly what he probably just did. She knew the Taylor grove consisted of considerable citrus acreage plus farmland. Her father was already acquainted with the men out there and had told the family about the place.

For the first time in her life, she had to collect her thoughts to focus on the thread in front of her instead of the man beside her. Sewing usually forced out other distractions.

"Well, first, what is the thread to be used for?" she asked.

"Dunno."

"No idea at all? For fancy work like embroidery? Or mending? Sewing fine clothes like church attire or heavy items such as denim work pants?"

He looked at her and she met a warm, open gaze in his brown eyes before he scrunched his face into a confused expression and shrugged his shoulders.

"I wasn't paying attention," he admitted. "Too busy thinking about my new saddle. Did you see it out there? Look, on my horse Maypop, the chestnut one right out there." He pointed through the glass windows that fronted the shop. The saddle on the horse tied to the hitching post appeared to Clara the same as any other saddle she'd ever seen.

"Uh, I see, yes, it's very nice," she said, in what she hoped was a tone of interest.

He laughed aloud.

"I'm guessing you know as much about saddles as I do about thread," Bill said.

Clara grinned. "It's that obvious?"

"No disrespect, but, yeah."

She laughed aloud. She wasn't sure why. But she was enjoying herself.

The fabric in the doorway divider rustled and Josefa returned with the chasuble folded and wrapped in a protective layer of muslin. She looked from Bill to Clara and back again and a gleam of interest grew in her eyes.

"Billy, perhaps Clara could return to the grove with you and find out exactly what's needed?" Josefa said. "I'd run out there myself but I'm a little busy right now."

The shop was empty except for the three of them.

The young man cleared his throat and spoke in a low tone. "Josefa, I go by Bill now, not Billy," he said. Clara tried to glance at him without him noticing. He did look more like a Billy than a Bill. But Bill sounded more sophisticated.

Bill spoke louder. "I'd be delighted to escort Miss DeForest." He turned to Clara.

"C'mon, you can ride out to the grove with me and check on the thread," he said. "Have you been to Taylor Grove yet? I don't think you have. Maypop is big enough to carry both of us."

Clara's eyes widened. These country people truly had no idea about society rules. He really expected her to ride out to the grove on the horse with him, alone? Not only was he a stranger, such physical closeness between men and women was frowned upon before betrothal or marriage. Now why did she just think of marriage? She inhaled and cleared her thoughts.

"I," she began, searching for the right words to say to these open-faced, welcoming people in front of her. She didn't want to offend them.

"I'd go, but—" Josefa interrupted, then stopped. A smile creased her face. "I waited so very long for God to grace me with this miracle that I dare not take any risks at all." She patted her abdomen.

Clara's gaze followed the movement and she saw the tiniest of swells. Her eyes widened as she lifted her gaze to meet Josefa's. Did women around here talk about pregnancy aloud, in public, and in front of unrelated men? What next?

"That's why I'm so busy," Josefa said. "Busy making baby things for my precious *bebita* or *bebé*. We'll find out in May. The little one will have enough clothing, diapers, bedding, and bibs to last a year or more by the time I'm finished."

"You feel the baby move yet?" Bill asked.

"Not yet, the but the doctor says I should, soon."

Clara felt a bit light-headed. The conversation was just so inappropriate for mixed company.

Her surprise must have shown on her face.

"Oh, dear, Clara, it's okay," Josefa said. "Billy is practically a brother to me and we're all a little more relaxed about things here. We're not that many years away from being a wilderness settlement, even though town has grown so much. Why, I remember when—"

Clara only half heard Josefa's reminiscences. She was stuck on how Josefa considered Persimmon Hollow to have grown so much. It was still a cow town. The streets were sand except for the main ones, which were paved with pine straw. A few blocks beyond town the wilderness was thick and, quite frankly, scary looking.

"You can best believe that when etiquette is called for, we're as proper as anyone else," Josefa added.

Clara stopped her internal stream of chatter. Honesty elbowed in. The light-headedness was more from the exertion of the walk than from the conversation. She also wasn't as shocked as she tried to tell herself she was. If anything, she was curious about Josefa's comment about waiting so long for a baby. Had Josefa, too, once been told she couldn't have children? If Josefa considered her pregnancy a miracle, maybe Clara could wish for the same in the future.

Clara looked from Josefa to Billy. Something about the two young people was comforting. She felt good standing in the shop with them. And if they were as close as brother and sister, well, no harm then in sibling-like conversations about delicate topics.

But Clara had her limits.

"Would it be okay if my sister went with us to the grove?"

she asked, knowing full well they'd need some kind of larger conveyance.

"Sure," Bill said. "Let me run over to the livery and borrow a cart. Then I'll carry you to your house and we'll get your sister. Wait here a few minutes, okay?"

He glanced back down at the thread on the counter. "Can I take some of these to show my mom and Lupita?" he asked Josefa.

Josefa nodded.

"Be right back," he said as he bolted out the door.

He returned just as Clara had finished selecting thread for the chasuble embroidery and Josefa was wrapping up the purchase. Gold for the cross, deep indigo for the grapes, golden brown for the wheat stalks, forest green for the grape leaves, and silver for the IHS letters.

Bill waved a magazine in his hand as he ran inside. "Wow, you two you won't believe this! Look, look at this ad for a Winton. I heard about them but this is the first I've seen one. Look at that picture! Boy, would I love to own one of them. Think how fast I could get around!"

Josefa and Clara peered at the open page to see what the fuss was about.

"Oh, I've seen one of those," Clara exclaimed as she looked at the picture of the car. "Back home, right before we moved. Our next-door neighbor bought one. He gave us all short rides in it. It was kind of scary. But fun, despite being so different." She'd been able to enjoy the sharp newness because it had been tempered by familiar people and surroundings.

Bill mock-groaned and grabbed at his chest. "Owww, I'm tortured by envy. Can I stand a little closer to you? It may be the closest I'll get to one of those cars."

He studied the ad again. "Then again, maybe not. I could siphon some of the money I'm saving for my fernery property and use it for a loan to buy a car. Yeah, I just might do that."

"And drive it on these roads?" Clara questioned, and pointed out the window. Thick, soft sand peeked out amid windblown and scattered pine straw. She remembered her ride in the car and couldn't imagine such a contraption puttering around this frontier.

Clara believed in facing reality and that others should, too. Even if she was having trouble accepting her new home.

"The tires would sink in the sand and get stuck," she said. "The car would sputter and stall. It wasn't a smooth ride even on city streets."

Bill studied the landscape and heaved a sigh. "Ouch. Thanks for the hard landing in the real world. One I guess I needed. You could say Persimmon Hollow isn't ready for a Winton. I can get a little carried away too quickly with new enthusiasms."

He scrutinized Clara's face with a new and deeper appraisal. "Your directness fits right in here," he said. "I'm glad you spoke up. I can't waste my hard-earned dollars on a folly. These vehicles are too new. But they sure are amazing. Gasoline-powered cars. Who would have thought."

He looked outside again. "Maypop is probably relieved I'm not running over to the bank to apply for a loan. You ready to go?" he asked Clara. "The wagon ain't as fast or fancy as an automobile but it'll get us there."

"Yes," Clara said. She hesitated, though, and considered walking rather than riding to the house with a young man she'd just met. What if he took off in the other direction?

"It's only a few blocks," Billy said. "You can practically see your house from here."

Alarm bells rang in Clara's mind.

"You know where I live? How?"

Bill took a step back. "Yes, but only because your dad and brother have been to the grove to talk with my dad and Josefa's Uncle Alfredo about citrus. Taylor Grove citrus is known throughout the state. Beyond that, even. Your Dad's grove has some of the same experimental trees my Dad invested in heavily a while back. They're the only trees that survived the Big Freeze."

"The freeze from a decade ago that everybody still talks about like it just happened?" Clara asked. "Half the trees on my Dad's small grove died. That's why he got it so cheap."

Bill's smile dimmed. "It was a bad time that wiped out some people's life savings. Others got discouraged and gave up. Like the man who sold to your Dad."

There was such a thing as being too direct, Clara reminded herself.

"I meant no disrespect," she said. "I didn't understand the severity of it. I just wish that man had kept his land so my Dad couldn't buy it and my family hadn't moved."

"To a place so different than what you're used to," Josefa said in a kind voice. "It must have been hard for you. My aunt and uncle live at the grove, too, and that's how we know about your family. We're all happy you're here."

She walked around the counter and handed Clara her package. "If you'd feel more comfortable, I'll stand outside and watch until I see Bill steer the wagon into your driveway."

Clara gave a weak laugh.

"Everything is just so different than city life," she said. "There, everything and everyone is suspect if you don't know them. Here, nothing and nobody seems to be."

"Only within certain circles of people," Bill said.

"Which you're a part of?" Clara half-asked.

He nodded.

Clara really didn't want to walk the three blocks home in the heat. Her whole body would rebel.

"You'll watch?" she asked Josefa.

She nodded.

"Okay, then," Clara said.

Bill grinned. "May I escort you to my fine carriage, miss?" he asked with a bow. He held out his arm.

Clara smiled at the description of the wooden cart as a carriage, and laid her hand on his arm. Josefa trailed them out of the shop, her smile growing wider by the minute.

Bill helped Clara onto the bench seat, climbed in, and eased the horse out into the road. "Too hot to ask her to move fast," he said to Clara, who perched on the far side of the wagon seat. "Especially when pulling a wagon."

She liked how he considered his horse's health.

"Not everybody would think of their horse like that," she commented.

"Nobody abuses an animal within miles of me," he said. "They're God's creatures as much as we are."

Clara liked Bill even more than she had upon first meeting him.

The drive to the house was short. Meg was out of the house and down the steps before they pulled to a stop.

"Why—what?!" She stopped short in her tracks. "I saw the strange wagon and came out and I have to say, I never expected to see you in it, Clara! What happened? Did you faint? Did you take ill? Is everything okay?" She looked at Bill with frank curiosity.

"Yes, everything's fine," Clara said. Was that how she acted, too? Questioning and possibly suspicious? It did seem a bit off-putting. She knew Meg was only concerned about her health, but Bill didn't know that.

"We need you to ride with us to Taylor Grove so Bill here can check what kind of thread his mother needs from the dress-maker," Clara told Meg. "I'm the expert going along to make sure he doesn't flub things again."

Meg stared as though a different person were inhabiting Clara's body and mind.

"You mean like a chaperone?" Meg asked.

"Exactly that," Bill said. "I'm Bill Taylor of Taylor Grove."

"Oh," Meg said. "Yes, I've heard Dad and Melvin and Harvey talk of your family. Let me check that Mama doesn't need me."

She soon returned, with a warmer reception in her tone of voice. "Mother is delighted that my sister is offering to help," she said with a pointed look at Clara. "And I'm excited to see the grove. I've heard much about it."

She climbed in the wagon, causing Clara to shift closer to Bill.

"Hi, I'm Meg," she said, and reached across Clara to shake Bill's hand, inadvertently pushing Clara even closer to Bill. Clara was acutely aware of the man next to her. She inched away as soon as she could so that her breath would slow down. It's just the heat, she told herself, that was making her out of breath.

Bill whistled as he turned the horse around and headed out to the grove.

The gentle breeze wove through the mix of dappled sunlight and shade as Bill guided the horse on a leisurely pace. Clara relaxed as the road curved and wound through homesteads and woods until turning onto the Taylor Grove property. The rows of citrus trees *were* pretty, she had to admit. And the temperature when in the shade was like a balmy cloak instead of a harsh reminder of where she was.

She tried to imagine herself huddled around a fireplace in the chill of winter up north. The picture wouldn't form. All that surfaced was the remembrance of how much her fingers chilled when she tried to crochet, no matter how close to the fire she was or how many hand and wrist warmers she put on. That certainly wasn't a problem here.

The screen door to a large log cabin opened with a crash

against the building as the wagon drew near the porch. A boy had shoved the door hard when he opened it and bolted out. Clara heard a woman's voice from within, admonishing "Seth Junior" to slow down.

"Billy! About time! You took long enough. Lemme see the saddle." Seth Junior galloped down the porch stairs and stopped short. "Huh? Where is it?"

Bill cast a sheepish glance toward Clara. "Guess I better admit I'm still 'Billy' around here. I'm working on getting people used to 'Bill' but not having much luck."

"Well, Bill does sound more grown up," Clara admitted as she gave him her hand to help her climb out and onto the mounting block. "But I can see you as a Billy."

"Good," he said and turned to the boy who was impatiently tugging on his shirt sleeve. "It's still in town, buddy," he told Seth Junior. "Ride back to town with us and you and I can come home on Maypop."

The boy's eyes shone. "That's a deal! Lemme tell them out in the grove that I'll be gone a while."

Clara frowned. "That young one works in the fields?" Oops, she'd meant only to think that, not say it. But her Aunt Hattie's protests about child labor in factories and on farms had popped into her mind. She clapped a hand over her mouth and felt Meg pinch her other hand.

"He shadows our father and wants to do every single job involved in citrus," Billy said, not the least bit offended. They watched Seth Junior disappear into a thicket.

Billy continued, "He'll grow into ownership of the citrus side of the family business, which will leave me to focus on the farming side and my main interest, fern growing. We learned to diversify more after the freeze hit citrus so hard. I've already started fernery experiments on land I'm in the process of buying. Glad I didn't get sidetracked on the car. Glad *you* helped me not get sidetracked, I mean...I have big plans. And everything will stay in the family. Can't get any better than that."

"You will stay here, in Persimmon Hollow?" Clara asked.

"Where else would I go?"

"Oh, a larger city, say, where there is more opportunity."

"Plenty of opportunity for this country boy right here."

Yes, Clara, she reminded herself. He's a country boy and you're a city girl. He's an outdoorsman and you're sentenced to a life of small, quiet movements. Nothing can develop between you even if your heart is starting to go pitter-patter near him.

"Why, hello, hello, come in!" A woman stood on the porch, two little girls by her side. Both were miniature versions of her. "Billy, where are your manners? Invite the young ladies inside for refreshments. You're the DeForest sisters, right?"

"They are," Billy answered for them. "They came to my rescue. You and Lupita befuddled me with the thread talk and I had to bring experts to find out exactly what you want." They climbed the porch stairs and moved toward the woman and girls.

Agnes Taylor made a quick round of introductions.

"I'm three," little Rosalia squeaked, and then hid behind her mother.

"And I'm six," said the taller Fannie, unafraid of the strangers.

"Three and six are good ages," Clara said. The little girls charmed her. And reminded her how she'd likely never be strong enough to bear a child. She pushed the thought away. Miracles did happen. Remember the dressmaker.

Young Seth re-emerged from the grove, bolted across the yard and clumped up each of the porch stairs with heavy steps. "Dad says okay," he yelled, although everyone was within a few feet of him.

"Good," Agnes said as she ushered everyone indoors. "Let's go have some tea while we go over the thread choices. The kettle is always on the stove."

"Sorry but I have to skip out on that," Billy quickly said. "Little Seth and I have some chores to do before we head back to town."

"Chores, what chores?" Seth protested. "Lemme go," he said, shaking off the hand Billy had placed on his shoulder. "I want that cinnamon cake Mama just made. I know she'll put it out with the tea."

"There are always chores around this place," Billy said, and headed for the door. "They can't top cake, I know. I'll be back in a bit."

"You'll miss cinnamon cake," his mother called after him.

"And thread talk!" he answered and flashed them his ready grin.

"He's always one to speak his mind," Agnes explained to Clara and Meg as the door closed behind Billy. "You always know where you stand with Billy. It's a good trait. But it surprises people sometimes upon first meeting him. I know it did me."

Ah, thought Clara as she took a seat at the dining room table and Agnes bustled into the kitchen. That might explain why Agnes looked way too young to be Billy's mother.

"I chaperoned Billy after he boarded the train I rode when I was moving to Persimmon Hollow years ago," Agnes answered Clara's unspoken question when she returned. She set down a tray containing a teapot, cups, plates, and a cake whose aroma scented the air with cinnamon and sugar. Agnes began serving and continued explaining.

"His aunt was sending Billy to live with his Uncle Seth here. Long story short, Seth and I eventually married and I gained an instant son. Seth gained an instant daughter in my adopted Polly. You'll soon meet her if you haven't already. She and Billy are close in age and both quite cheeky in their behavior sometimes. Seth and I also have three little ones, Seth Junior, who's ten, and Rosalia and Fannie, who already shared their ages."

The two little girls sat side-by-side and giggled.

Clara saw the depth of love in the glance Agnes cast her young son and daughters.

"Enough about me," Agnes said. "Tell me about yourself."

"There's not much to say about me," Clara said. "I'm twenty-two and I lead a quiet life. Meg is twenty-four and getting married next year. How old are Polly and Billy?" She didn't want to talk about herself. Those conversations always ended up focused on her delicate health.

"Clara!" chided Meg.

"I was just wondering!" Clara said. Innocent question, she told herself. She wasn't being rude. Curious, that's all. But she was somewhat surprised at herself. It was her second inappropriate question within minutes. She wasn't usually so unsettled. Billy's image floated into her mind. She pushed it away, unwilling to admit he was the distraction.

"Polly is twenty-three and teaches botany at the Academy," Agnes said. "She's in the early stages of a courtship with a professor at the College there, praise the Lord. She's an independent one, my Polly. And Billy is twenty-four."

Agnes looked at Clara for a long moment and smiled. "He doesn't have a girlfriend, in case you're interested. I'd be overjoyed to see him settle down. He's overdue. All he does is work."

Clara almost choked on her tea. She questioned if the sunny climate had addled her. She was starting to act as casually as the other people in Persimmon Hollow and Agnes had noticed. She'd probably overheard Clara's comment about young Seth's work habits. Then Clara had rudely asked people's ages. Now Billy's mother assumed she fit right in with country life and started dropping big hints.

Oh, Clara, she moaned to herself, you're losing your city refinements already.

"I just wondered because—" Clara tried to explain. There was no explanation. Her voice trailed off.

"Might want to stop while you're ahead," Meg leaned over and whispered. Clara pursed her lips. Meg struggled not to laugh.

"I'm just happy to see you interested in something," Meg said. She directed her next comment to Agnes.

"Clara has been having a hard time adjusting since our move to Persimmon Hollow."

"You poor dear," Agnes said to Clara. "I understand. I was so homesick at first. But Persimmon Hollow and its people and this beautiful grove worked their magic on me."

"Along with your handsome husband," said a man who'd just come in the back door.

"Papa!" cried Rosalia, and raised her hands for him to lift her. Fannie jumped up and ran over for a hug. Young Seth waved but remained focused on devouring his snack.

"Got any of that cake left?" Seth asked as he kissed his wife, tousled his son's hair, picked up Rosalie, and pulled Fannie close to his side.

"For you, always," Agnes said, and introduced him to Clara and Meg.

*Read Agnes and Seth's story in At Home in Persimmon Hollow
(Persimmon Hollow Legacy Series, Book 1)*

Clara sensed the love that filled the room. What a delightful family, she thought.

"Give this town and all of us a chance, Clara," Agnes said to her. "You might be surprised."

Maybe so, thought Clara. But part of her doubted it.

About an hour later, Billy, now accompanied by Seth Junior, drove Clara and Meg back into town. They stopped at the dress-maker's, where Clara explained exactly what kind of thread Billy needed to bring home. He insisted on driving her and Meg the short distance to the DeForest house.

"It's the least I can do for your help," he said to Clara.

He hopped out first when they reached the house, and helped Clara and Meg out before waving a cheery farewell and driving off.

"You're actually smiling," Meg said to Clara as they strolled up the walkway.

Yes, she was, Clara thought. And it felt good.

PART II

December 4, 1898

Advent, Week Two—Peace

Clara spied a letter for her on the side table when she came in from picking camellia flowers on a blissfully cool day. She plopped down the cut flowers, peeled off her gardening gloves, and snatched the letter as though afraid it would fly off.

"Who's it from?" Meg asked as she followed Clara indoors and picked up the flowers before they dirtied the table. "I'll put these in a vase."

"It's from Beth! It probably has wedding details," Clara sang out as Meg headed toward the kitchen.

Clara sat down on the foyer chair and opened the envelope. How exciting it must be up there, with all the preparations swirling around, she thought. All the pre-wedding festivities she was missing.

Her cheerfulness from being out amid flowers in delicious temperatures seeped away with each sentence of the letter. She'd missed a bridesmaid luncheon, an afternoon sleigh excursion, and a candlelight concert. She read about wedding rehearsal details, floral bouquet ideas, table décor decisions, and color schemes. She learned that a small storm had blown through and dusted the trees and yards and roads with sparkling snow that was soft and beautiful.

The letter ended with a plea: *"Ask your mother if you may arrive a week earlier! You can spend Christmas with us!! We all miss you so much!"*

Shouting startled Clara out of her thousand-mile daydream.

"Hey, move along, git, move along!" she heard Melvin yell outside. Melvin shouted again and Clara heard Meg's boyfriend, Harvey, guffaw.

Clara got up and walked out onto the porch to see what the commotion was about. Palm trees, sandy paths, and oak limbs laden with Spanish moss reminded her where she was.

There, in the roadway in front of the house, stood a large cow, nose-to-nose with her brother's cart. The cart was sideways, as though Melvin had tried to steer around the animal but didn't have enough room. Melvin and Harvey stood on the floorboards, waving their arms and yelling at the animal. The immobile bovine stared at them and snorted.

The standoff continued for what seemed long minutes. Then, a man on horseback galloped into view. He hollered for "Daisy" and yelled at Melvin and Harvey to quit messing with his cow.

The horse rider halted next to Daisy, which seemed to give him some kind of greeting. Clara wondered if cows knew their owners. The rider was skinny, with long hair and an unruly beard. His clothing was worn and dusty and his Stetson hat had seen better days. He spat into the roadway and yawned.

"C'mon here, Daisy," he said and leaned over and placed a loose rope around the cow's neck. The animal nudged him and went willingly.

"Much obliged," the man said to Melvin and Harvey as he

and the cow turned around and ambled back up the road. Melvin and Harvey stared, open mouthed.

Clara's mouth was closed, her lips compressed so tightly they almost hurt. Maybe she could head north early. Maybe she could head north tomorrow.

"No, your mother and I don't think it's a good idea," her father, Orville DeForest, said at the dinner table that evening. After she'd worked up the nerve to make the request about going north ahead of time. Clara tried not to frown. Papa's word was law and was doubly strong when combined with Mama's. Clara occasionally had luck convincing one of them about the value of whatever she was asking for, but not when they were united against it.

Still, she had to give it a try.

"It's only for one extra week," she said, and took a bite of sweet potato. Now wasn't the time to bring up her idea of living permanently with Aunt Hattie. Her aunt was so nonconformist that Clara feared she'd receive a resounding "No!" if she raised the question now. She also wondered herself how her tidy, organized daily habits would fit with her aunt's looser lifestyle.

"I know it's only an extra week, but you must consider your health, dear," Gertrude DeForest said to Clara. "I'm concerned about you being gone even for ten days. It's a strenuous journey and you'll have scant time to rest amid the wedding festivities. Long hours of travel each way and busy days of activity in between. I've half a mind to suggest you beg your excuses."

"No, Mama!" Clara blurted. "My health is fine right now!"

"It's been better since we moved here," Meg piped in.

"Yes, I've noticed the same," their mother said.

"I knew moving to Persimmon Hollow was a good idea," their father said.

Clara's spirits drooped. The windows rattled as if to accentuate her inner dismay. The balmy day had chilled a few hours earlier and turned gray and blustery. The conversation shifted to her brother's retelling of the cow-and-cart episode. Her father shook his head good-naturedly, Meg laughed aloud and even her mother seemed amused.

Her brother glanced at what Clara knew was her sour expression.

"Sorry we're boring you, little one."

"I'm twenty-two years old!" Clara snapped at her older brother. "I'm not a sickly child anymore. I'm not 'little one.' I'm just short. Stop babying me! The only thing I'm sick of is everybody coddling me!" Her volume had inched upward with each sentence.

All activity at the table quieted.

"Except your sickly childhood has reached into your adulthood," her mother gently reminded her. "You almost died from whooping cough. Your twin sister did die. I know you were too young to remember. But the infection settled deep in you and weakened your lungs. At times you could hardly breathe. Your lungs will always be fragile. It's a fact you must accept and live with. Oh, darling, be grateful you're alive. We are."

"You also may want to seek God's forgiveness for your rude outburst, through Confession," her father said. "Perhaps some contemplation during home prayer and at Mass can help you accept what you can't change," he added.

They finished the rest of the meal in silence.

As Clara helped clear the table, her mother, still somber, turned to her. "I hope you'll join us at the church cleanup tomorrow. You can't exert yourself but you can be sociable, especially when we gather for the picnic lunch afterwards. We want to have the church sparkling before the Feast of the Immaculate Conception. Gaudete Sunday is only a few days after that. How are you coming along on the embroidery?"

"Oh, just fine. Of course I'll join you tomorrow," Clara said quickly. She wouldn't be much help with the physical chores, but she'd bring the chasuble and continue stitching on the embroidery. She wasn't anywhere near being finished but didn't want to admit she might need help. Embroidery was one of the few things she *could* do. She gulped and tamped down a nudge of anxiety. She had time yet. No need to panic.

Small, wooden Persimmon Hollow Catholic Church was pretty in a quaint way, Clara had to admit. She liked how the sun poured through the oval stained-glass window situated above the front door. It cast warm color into the church. Clear light from the windows on each side of the building added brightness.

She dusted the church's statues, including her favorite of the Holy Family gazing down on a table of votive remembrance candles. Then she sat down near one of the windows and withdrew her embroidery from the canvas bag she'd brought.

She focused on her work. Murmurs of the other women cleaning the altar and pews and washing the floor faded into the background. The satin stitches for the cross and IHS letters were taking forever. Clara willed her fingers to pick up speed. So much remained undone. She hadn't even started the wheat stalks yet or the grapes. At least the outline of grape leaves was completed. But even that would look better with some embellishment.

The door banged open and she jumped, startled, and turned to see who'd arrived. Everyone else stopped work for the moment, too.

"Oops about that and sorry I'm late," Billy said. He angled a ladder through the doorway and perched it next to the door. "It won't take me long to get this window cleaned." He gestured toward the stained glass window high on the wall above the door.

"I hope none of you ladies attempted it," he added, and looked around the room.

"Hey!" he said when he saw Clara. His face brightened. Clara's breathing picked up. She smiled.

"What are you working on?" he asked, and loped over to her.

"It's a good time for a short break," Agnes Taylor called out.

"Clara, show Mrs. Taylor and the others the chasuble embroidery," Gertrude DeForest said. "I'm sure they'd love to see it."

Clara looked down at her work as she heard footsteps echo off the wooden floor and then stop near her. She quickly positioned the fabric so that the neatest, most complete section of embroidery showed.

"How beautiful," Agnes said. The others echoed her, including Billy.

"Clara does fine work," Gertrude said. "How is your timing, Clara? Should any of us get ready to help? We're all willing."

The other woman echoed their support. Clara stiffened. She didn't want Billy or anyone to consider her a weakling—someone who always needed assistance because she was so frail. She was determined to finish the embroidery herself.

"No, I should be okay," she said, and pasted a smile on her face. She slid a hand over the fabric to ensure nothing would slip and expose how much remained unfinished.

"As long as you're certain," her mother said.

"From what I already know about your daughter, ma'am, she'll be good on her word," Billy said in her defense.

Clara cast him a grateful look.

Agnes and Gertrude exchanged glances.

"Ma, can I share in the picnic goodies you brought for everyone if I get that window done pronto?" Billy asked.

Agnes laughed. "Of course! Although it's the first time I've seen you interested in joining ladies for lunch."

Billy slid a glance at Clara and grinned.

She sent one back.

"I have my reasons," he said.

By noon, chores were complete and the church sparkled. Everyone filtered outdoors into the shifting, dappled shade underneath tall pines. Clara was struck by how heavenly the air felt. Cool yet nice. A Florida version of winter, she realized. Far better than a cold snowy wind would feel at that moment. She felt good. No shortness of breath or fatigue. Just an uplifting, pleasant sense of contentment.

Billy sat next to Clara on an outstretched quilt while the older women sat on benches around a rectangular slab of wood supported by brick pillars.

She nibbled on bread slathered with a jelly she'd never tasted before. "Mmm, this is good."

"Like it?" Billy asked. "It's persimmon jelly."

She nodded her appreciation and kept eating.

"Polly and I are going out to the big spring south of town to pick more persimmons tomorrow if you want to come with us. We can canoe if this good weather holds. We can paddle along the spring run and see if any of the manatees are in."

She raised an eyebrow in question and to avoid answering. Canoe? Her? She'd be out of breath after a few paddles.

"What are manatees?" she asked instead.

"Sea cows. They cluster in the warmer spring water when the river chills down. Hundreds of them come in to the spring run every winter. They're a sight. Big, blubbery, docile things that roll around and surface every so often to breathe. I guarantee you've never seen anything like them. Still a little early for them. The weather hasn't been really cold enough yet. But we can check."

"You've got my interest," she said. "But I don't know how to canoe."

"It's easy," he said. "I'll teach you."

She wanted, very much, to go. With him.

"C'mon," he said. "Your sister and her boyfriend might want to come too. Polly won't miss it. She doesn't have a class scheduled until afternoon."

Should she tell him she lacked the stamina needed for such an excursion? When she really wanted to go? No, Clara decided. For once, she wanted to act normal and be like everyone else.

"I'd love to go," she said. "And I think my sister and her fiancé will, too."

"We'll be at your house right after sunrise tomorrow," Billy said. "Early morning is the best time to see manatees."

Clara saw her mother in a quiet conversation with Agnes Taylor. They both turned and looked at her and Billy briefly, then resumed their chat.

Clara spent the rest of her day on the porch at home, embroidering on the chasuble and doing her breathing exercises. She had been neglecting them of late. Forgetting them, actually. She was finding she didn't need them as much.

Clara wrapped the quilt more tightly around her shoulders and peered through the morning fog. The world looked magical, shrouded in a mist that softened the sharp edges of the trees' pine needles and the palmetto fronds that spiked upward from rounded bases. Birdcall familiar and new carried through the air.

Billy turned off the main pine straw road onto a narrow sandy path littered with shells. They crunched as the wheels rolled over them.

He craned his neck and peered upward as they passed under tree canopy.

"What's up there?" Clara asked.

"Looking for mistletoe," he said and gave her a grin that grew wider when he took in her expression.

Was he making a joke? She wasn't sure. Who would hang mistletoe high in a tree in the middle of a country pathway? Clara realized how little she really knew about Billy. Had he snuck out here hours ago to tie mistletoe in trees, so he could boldly try to steal a kiss?

Her imagination whirred and tumbled with her uncertainties about the unfamiliar locale and the new people in it.

She was glad Meg, Harvey, and Billy's sister Polly were in the seat behind them. She cast a sideways glance at Billy.

"Puh-leeze," exclaimed Polly in a loud voice. "The least you can do is explain yourself, Billy."

"You can't see the look on Clara's face from back there," he said.

Clara drew herself up straighter and stared ahead. Bill, Billy, whatever he was called, was behaving strangely.

"Oh, okay," Billy said, seconds later. "I won't leave you in suspense. Wouldn't want someone to do it to me. Mistletoe grows on these trees naturally," he said, and pointed upward. "See the globe-like growths?"

Clara peered skyward and actually did see the growths.

"That's mistletoe? Truly?"

"Uh huh. The stuff you saw hanging in doorways up north came from places like this." He grew more animated. "There's so much to discover around here and I'm happy to show it all to you."

She didn't answer. She didn't want to become too fond of or familiar with Persimmon Hollow. Yet she liked Billy and was starting to feel a bond with him. She pursed her lips. This new development interfered with her determination to continue thinking of Persimmon Hollow as a temporary residence.

"When you're ready, that is," Billy added. "I don't mean to press. I get excited about stuff and want to share things with everyone."

"What he's really saying is he's sorry he has no patience,"

Polly called from the back seat. "But I can vouch for him being a good guy, even if he's an annoying brother sometimes."

They all laughed and the morning returned to its easy rhythm. The path narrowed and then opened into a clearing.

Before them lay a scene Clara knew she'd remember for the rest of her life. A small pool of water the color of an aquamarine gemstone shimmered in an earthen basin. Tangled ferns, shrubs, vines, and trees grew around the edges except for one open space where white sand sloped down to meet the water. The shallow water at the edge was so transparent she could almost count the grains of sand and strands of willowy aquatic grass underneath.

Her gaze followed the water from the round basin out into a narrow channel that merged with the river some distance beyond. Patches of mist hovered over the spring run and added a dreamy softness to the view. The air was soft.

"This is one of the most beautiful places of God's creation I've ever seen," she whispered.

"You understand!" Billy also spoke in a low voice.

"Oh, yes."

He exhaled slowly, as though relieved she also felt the mystery and beauty of this hidden corner of the earth.

"Is this where the manatees are?" she asked.

"Yeah, all along the spring run, but I don't see any. They'll be here for sure next month and in February. We'll come back out then."

She didn't say she wouldn't be here. But a tiny crack rippled through her resolve to leave Persimmon Hollow.

"I'd still like to take you out in the canoe right now, if you're agreeable," he said. He looked over his shoulder to the others. "Canoe?"

"What are we waiting for?" Polly said and scrambled out of the wagon, followed by Meg and Harvey. Billy was on the ground and by Clara's side before Polly had even finished speaking. He helped her out as though she were a fragile leaf in danger of fluttering or breaking.

"Here, we store canoes in the brush," he said, and pointed toward a thicket.

A short while later, he and Clara were in one canoe and Polly, Meg, and Harvey in the other. They glided along the quiet waterway. An anhinga perched on a low tree branch with its wings spread out to dry.

"I managed to get in and sit down without tipping the canoe over," Clara said, happy with her meager outdoor skills. She gazed at Billy from her front bench seat.

"That you did," Billy said. "You're almost an expert already."

A smile creased her face.

Billy pointed out underwater caves as they moved out over the mouth of the spring. Clara stared in awe at the rocky limestone formations. They appeared tinted blue from the water, which was so clear she could see depressions in the sand far below, where small bubbles burst upward. Water gushed from between the rocks and gurgled toward the surface.

Billy steered them down the spring run. He paddled and guided the boat's movements with such expertise that they glided over the water with barely a ripple. His paddle made a gentle lapping sound each time he scooped it in and out of the water. Clara grew relaxed and drowsy. She wanted to lie down and stare up at the sky.

"Want to try paddling?" Billy asked, then peered closely at her. "You don't have to. Your eyes are half-closing. If you want, sit in the canoe bottom and rest your head against the bench. Use my jacket as a pillow. Just enjoy the ride."

"Thanks," she said, and rearranged herself without tipping the vessel. She was glad to escape paddling and the inevitable questions that would arise when she grew out of breath after a few minutes. Her eyelids felt heavy. The weather, the water, the breeze, the sun and sky—the company—made her want to prolong the excursion as long as possible.

She was in that relaxed state between wakefulness and sleep when a thump from below the canoe startled her fully awake.

"Whoa, fellow, move along." Billy was tense and alert. He held his paddle above the water with one hand. With the other, he reached under his seat and pulled out a long item wrapped in layers of fabric. He laid the bundle across his lap.

"Git!" he shouted, and banged the side of the canoe with a fist. Clara jerked in surprise. Eyes wide, she looked to see what he was dealing with. She came almost face to face with a broad, flat head, and long, toothy snout on a scaly creature that seemed to grin at her.

"Oh my, oh my," was all she could utter. She withdrew her hands from where she'd gripped the canoe's edge when first awakened. She scrambled back up onto the seat. Her knees knocked together from trembling.

"It's okay," Billy said.

But it wasn't. She saw him unwrap the fabric and withdraw a shotgun.

His glance followed her gaze. "A precaution," he said. "Last resort."

The alligator remained motionless and Billy started to quietly and quickly paddle back away from it.

"Gators don't bother folks unless we're near their nest or they've lost their fear of humans cause people fed them," he said, never taking his gaze off the reptile. "Not sure what's up with this one. Too early for nesting season. Not many folks live around here and they know better than to feed a gator. Gotta be tourists. Trophy hunters. Rich guys who camp out for weeks to hunt and fish up and down the river in fall and winter. Some might have fed gators, trying to lure one close for an easy shot. This gator sure gave us a strong bump. Sending a message."

"What is it saying?"

"Maybe that we're too close to its territory," Billy said. "They got a right to this place, too. I'm actually glad this one escaped the trophy hunters. But if it keeps acting aggressive the game warden's gonna have to dispatch him."

His humor returned the farther they distanced themselves from the alligator, which didn't pursue them. Billy stopped paddling, rewrapped the shotgun and replaced it under the seat.

"We live in a place surrounded by wilderness and critters," he said. "I dislike taking an animal's life but will do so to protect myself and my lov—my friends and family. That's the first time I got bumped like that. He was a huge one. A ten-footer, at least. You can tell by the distance between the eyes."

Clara nodded, but the day's magic was gone. Florida's weirdness was on full display. Why did such perfection as the spring waters have to be marred by threats from prehistoric looking creatures with toothy mouths as wide as their heads?

"Can we go back now?" she asked, her voice small.

"Yeah, we gotta pick persimmons, anyway," he said. "I promise it'll be less intense."

The smell of the fruit sweetened the ride back to town, but Clara couldn't shake the remembrance of the alligator encounter. The others chatted about it as though it had been a great adventure. She hardly wanted a life of such adventures. Or of wilderness and critters.

Another shock awaited Clara at home. Meg and Harvey, too, stopped in their tracks as they all walked indoors after Billy and Polly dropped them off.

There, at the kitchen table, sat Aunt Hattie with Mother. Meg and Harvey offered quick hellos and made a hasty exit.

Clara checked off the days in her mind. Her letter to Aunt

Hattie couldn't have arrived yet, much less given her aunt time to answer or hustle down to Florida. Why was she here?

Aunt Hattie was a longtime widow whose husband and two children had perished in a yellow fever epidemic. She had grieved far longer than anyone expected and then refused to remarry. Had even taken back her maiden name. She emerged from mourning with a strong voice and large opinions that belied her petite size. Aunt Hattie belonged to the hometown suffragette club and regularly debated the parish priest about the church's disapproval of women casting ballots. She ventured into the less savory sides of their home city to help people she called "the less fortunate" and was a ceaseless voice for better treatment of factory and sweatshop workers.

Clara's father pleaded with his sister to stay home and knit or crochet items for charity, but made no headway. Clara's mother tried to interest Hattie in charitable fundraisers. Aunt Hattie preferred to help firsthand. "Nothing more boring than society matrons one-upping each other around tables laden with enough food to feed an entire tenement for a week," she'd once exclaimed. Loudly.

Oh, dear, Clara thought. Acting that way in a city was one thing. Would Aune Hattie start pontificating and crossing boundaries here, too? Clara could imagine living with her amid the bustle of the city. But not here. Just as quickly, she wondered at her sudden protective attitude toward Persimmon Hollow.

And with Aunt Hattie here, Clara couldn't stay with her up north for that extra week she still hoped to claim. Not that her parents had approved that plan, though.

"My doctor's been after me for years to move to a warmer climate," Aunt Hattie said. "So I've come to see what this place is about. Don't worry, child," she added to Clara. "We'll travel north together in enough time for you to get to that wedding. I had a notion to see this town and time's a'wastin.'"

"Your telegram arrived almost the same time you did,"

Clara's mother said, and rubbed her temple. "But we're delighted you're here." Clara met her mother's gaze. They all loved Hattie, but the small woman's intensity steamrolled the quieter souls around her. The family's routine was about to be upset in a major way.

"I've been waiting for you, Clara," Aunt Hattie said and rose from the table. "You can show me around. Let's go. Oh, posh, don't look at me like a fainting lily. You'll never get strong if you act like an invalid. In fact, you appear far more healthful than last time I saw you. The warmth and outdoors here must be beneficial."

Clara surprised herself. "I really must embroider on a chasuble Mother asked me to complete for Gaudete Sunday," she said to her aunt. "Perhaps after lunch you'd like to sit with me on the porch as I work? I've already been out all morning, canoeing on the river."

Aunt Hattie appeared impressed at Clara's gumption. "Well, then," she said, and sat back down.

"Yes, and we even saw an alligator. Close up."

"Indeed! I declare there's hope for you yet."

Aunt Hattie fanned herself while Clara embroidered. The sun rode high and had blazed away the delightful morning air. The porch's shade offered a modicum of relief.

Clara's eyelids drooped. She jerked awake when her head bobbed down.

"That morning expedition sapped more of my energy than I thought," she said to her aunt, who waved away the excuse.

"No reason to apologize. I can't tell you how delighted I am to see you taking part in life."

"What do you mean? I've always been active."

Aunt Hattie snorted. "You and your family use your weak

health to cushion you far too much. You're like a turtle afraid to come out of its shell."

Meg had strolled out to the porch in time to hear Hattie's last sentence.

"You should have seen her a month or two ago. The turtle was not only in its shell, it had retreated into its burrow."

"Is that so?" Aunt Hattie peered at Clara.

"But I think she's sweet on a guy named Billy, the one who dropped us off before," Meg continued. "She has stopped sulking around the house. She's done more in recent days than in recent months."

Clara's impatience tugged at her. "Neither of you understand what it's like. You don't have to determine whether you have enough breath to do something. Or whether you'll get winded to the point of gasping for air or fainting. As far as being a turtle, you'd never say that if you knew what was in the letter I mailed to you, Aunt Hattie, a short while ago."

Neither woman answered her.

Clara looked from one to the other. Hattie raised her eyebrows.

"And the letter said what?" her aunt asked.

Meg plopped down next to Clara in the cushioned porch swing. "We're waiting," she said, and pushed the railing with her foot so the swing rocked.

"You can't tell Mama or Papa yet," Clara said, with a glance at the closed front door. "Aunt Hattie, I want to come live permanently with you up north. I'll never grow to like it here."

And I'm afraid if I stay I'll grow more attached to Billy and won't want to leave, she didn't say. From deeper inside came the unwelcome fear that Billy's interest might cool once he knew the extent of her health issues. Better to move back home and avoid the inevitable disappointment.

Meg planted her feet on the floor and halted the swing.

"You can't do that!" she exclaimed.

Hattie's expression betrayed nothing. "The big question is why do it?" Hattie said. "And I make no promises of silence."

"Me either," said Meg, and crossed her arms over her chest.

"It's backwards here," Clara said. "The city is more cultured. My friends are there. The people here are so hardy and pioneer-like. I don't fit in. They talk too frankly about delicate matters. And go on and on about citrus growing and something called ferneries and, why, there's not even a museum here. And cows wander in the streets!"

Meg stared at her older sister. "Mama and Papa won't even let you add an extra week to your trip for Beth's wedding. They'll never let you move back up there by yourself."

"They might if I live with Aunt Hattie."

"Sorry to disillusion you, dear, but I'm considering moving here," Hattie said. "I don't particularly like the newness of this place either. But life is what we make of it. As you, above all people, already know."

Not the answer Clara wanted to hear. Plus, her comment about ferneries had planted the thought of Billy into her mind. The image refused to budge.

The thump of horse hooves on sand broke the silence that draped the porch after Aunt Hattie's gentle admonition. Clara would have welcomed any diversion but seeing Billy ride up with Polly seated behind him was the best she could have wished for.

She set her embroidery on the side table, brushed imaginary wrinkles out of her skirt and patted her hair before Billy and Polly had a chance to jump off Maypop and climb the porch steps.

Meg gave a small snort and Aunt Hattie's eyes widened in interest.

"Hi," Billy said. "Mom was going to wait until tomorrow to come into town and ask you guys but I had a break from chores and offered to ride in and deliver the message," he said in one rapid clip. He ran a hand through his hair as he looked at Clara.

He looked both so manly and boyish at the same time. Clara's spirits, sagging from the earlier conversation, brightened so much she had to accept the inevitable truth. She was falling for this country boy. Instead of being upset that he interfered with her plans, she actually felt happy when she looked at him.

"My class was canceled so I came along for the ride," Polly said.

"How do you do, young man, young lady, I'm Clara and Meg's Aunt Hattie," Hattie said.

"Pleased to meet you, ma'am," Billy and Polly said.

"Oh, where are my manners?" exclaimed Clara. She hurriedly made full introductions, inwardly astonished at her *faux pas*.

"Your manners were overtaken by dreams of your new beau," said Meg, low enough for only Clara to hear. Clara elbowed her and Meg giggled.

"You were speaking of a question of some kind, young man?" Hattie asked Billy.

"Yeah," he said, and pulled himself straighter as he turned toward Hattie. "My mother wanted to have a Christmas choir but our congregation isn't large enough to do Midnight Mass justice. She just got word that both the Methodists and Baptists offered to help. They have some mighty good singers. Time's short but Mom's scheduling rehearsals for next week. She hopes all of you will join us."

He'd spoken the last words while looking straight at Clara.

"That sounds like fun!" Meg said. "I think I can speak for my family and say yes. Mama hums all the time and Papa has a fine voice. We can all carry a tune."

"I'll be there," Hattie said. "I believe in diving in to new situations and places as quickly as possible."

Only Clara remained silent. Her singing voice was marginal.

She tended to cough at the end of every long note and grow winded before a song's second verse. She glanced sideways at Meg, who returned a worried look. Hattie also looked at her, but gave away nothing. All knew it was impossible to urge, charm, or cajole Clara's breath into sustaining the exertion required of a choir member.

Billy looked at her with questioning eyes, as though he could feel her hesitation.

"You sing, right?" he asked.

Clara toyed with the lace on her sleeve cuff.

"Oh, I've got to go!" Meg said. "I have to meet Harvey. Polly, come say hello to Mother." She rose and hurried inside with Polly, the door closing behind them before the porch swing stopped squeaking.

"I'd better see if your mother needs assistance with dinner," said Hattie, who long ago had been banned from kitchen duty because she interfered more than helped. "Stay here a while," she said to Clara and headed inside. "The fresh air is good for you."

Billy kept looking at Clara as the door clicked close and the porch swing stilled.

"You're a very outdoorsy person, rugged and healthy," Clara began, her gaze averted.

"Yeah, that's me. You'll be too, soon, the longer you live here."

Thank you, Lord, Clara inwardly prayed, for giving me an easy opening for this awkward conversation.

"No, I won't, and that's what I need to tell you," she said, and her gaze met his.

Billy's open, happy face clouded.

"I know this isn't my business but I have to ask. Are you ill?"

"In a way," Clara said. She tugged on her inner resolve. If he galloped away after hearing of her health issues, well, at least their budding relationship would end before growing too deeply. Before changing her set-in-stone moving plan.

He pulled a chair opposite her and sat down. He braced his arms on his thighs and clasped his hands together.

"How can I help?"

That wasn't the question she expected. Her heart warmed toward him. A peaceful feeling settled on her, as though she could tell him anything and it would be okay.

"Nobody can help, Billy," she said. "I almost died as a child, from whooping cough. The illness affected my lungs. I could live to be a hundred but never have the breathing capacity of a healthy person. It's one reason why I struggle to adapt here. Everything, everyone, here is so vigorous and hardy. I have to lead a quiet life – sewing, reading, drawing. I was helping form plans for a new museum before moving down here. I can attend the theater and go to museums but I'll never be able to paddle a canoe like you, or walk great distances or—"

"Clara," he said, and reached out and placed his hand over hers.

She widened her eyes and parted her lips but remained silent.

"If I've heard it once I've heard it a hundred times from my parents and the Sisters at the orphanage and Father at Mass," Bill said. "The Lord gives each one of us gifts. We use them to the best of our ability. So you can't sing as long or as loudly as others. So what? Just come and keep us company as we rehearse. I guarantee the longer you live here the more you'll find an outlet for your special gifts."

She wasn't sure what to say. She should tell him she planned to move back home. But it would break this special moment. And she didn't want it to end.

"If it's all right with you and your family, I repeat my offer of introducing you to the wonders of Florida," Billy said. "We'll adapt, that's all. Make it work for you."

Clara's heart was touched.

"You don't mind carting around a semi-invalid?" she asked. A cautious note crept in before she could turn it off.

"Nah," he said, and the sunny Billy was back. "I got more than enough energy and strength for us both."

Two hawks soared over the porch, one after the other, calling to each other. In the distance, cardinals chirped.

"I do love all the birds here," Clara said.

"Wait until you see a sandhill crane," he said. "In spring you see the parents with one or two of their little ones, they're called colts, strolling around like little families. The parents mate for life."

Was he saying something to her, Clara wondered. Sending some message? But he had risen and now stood at the porch railing. He leaned over and searched the skies.

"The red-shouldered hawks are majestic, too," he continued, as though mating were the furthest thing from his mind. "I was hoping they'd swoop back around toward us but they're gone."

Clara remembered what his mother and sister said about Billy speaking his mind. He jumped from one subject to another without a care.

The door opened and they both turned to see Mrs. DeForest, Meg, Aunt Hattie, and Polly stroll out.

"Tell your mother we're honored to be part of the choir," Gertrude DeForest said. "It's wonderful news. When is the first rehearsal?"

"Next Tuesday," Billy said. "At church."

"We'll be there," Gertrude said. "All of us. Clara can help by singing as much as she is able."

"She'll help just by being there," Billy said.

"I'll bring my embroidery, too," Clara said, and indicated the chasuble.

"Oh, do show Polly your progress," her mother said.

Clara almost grimaced. She should have kept her mouth shut. Now she was stuck. Nobody knew how far behind she was, not even her mother. She'd mumbled vague assurances every time her mother mentioned it. She hated asking for help.

"Clara?" her mother prodded.

Clara appealed to her mother through her eyes. Gertrude returned a calm, steady gaze. A knowing gaze.

"Yes, mother," she mumbled.

Maypop whinnied and Billy excused himself to check on the horse. Thank goodness, Clara thought. She didn't want Billy to see her near-failure-in-the-making.

"That's some nice work," Polly said, when Clara displayed the embroidered portion of the chasuble.

"Beautiful, like everything Clara embroiders," Meg said.

"Is that for Gaudete Sunday?" Aunt Hattie asked. "It's pink, it must be."

Clara nodded.

"Beauty and all the ability in the world won't finish that by Sunday," said Aunt Hattie.

Leave it to Aunt Hattie. And she wanted to live with her?

"Clara, I'll help," Meg said. "No arguments."

"Your aunt and I will, too," Gertrude added.

"Count me out, sorry," said Polly. "You'd have to redo anything I stitched. But I know my mother will be here in a heartbeat soon as I mention it. When are you going to do this?"

"The sooner the better," Gertrude said. "Clara, what if we all commit to helping for a few hours tomorrow afternoon?"

"I, uh, couldn't—" began Clara, then almost bit her lip in shutting up. Accept this offer of help and friendship, you mule, she told herself.

"I would be ever so grateful," she said. "And honored." Again, a peace settled on her, as though everything were falling into a place she hadn't fathomed she wanted.

"I'll lower and adjust the quilting frame," Gertrude said. "With all of us stitching, we'll be finished in no time at all."

Billy bounded back up onto the porch. "You ready, Polly?

We gotta get back. I'll let Mom know about the choir," he said to Gertrude. "Thanks!" His gaze swept over them all but lingered on Clara's for a few moments longer. Then he and Polly climbed onto Maypop and galloped off.

The man was bold and bright as the sun that swept over the landscape, Clara decided. A sunlight she enjoyed seeing.

"I believe we have a courtship in the making," declared Aunt Hattie.

Clara felt the blood rising to her face.

"In such a—what did you call it—a *backwards* place," Meg said to Clara. "You might even change your mind and stick around."

Their mother glanced from one to the other but didn't comment on Meg's statement. Clara met her mother's gaze. She saw love and understanding in her eyes and a smile in her expression.

The next day, the women joined forces and completed the embroidery. Agnes arrived with her friend and housekeeper Lupita and with Josefa the dressmaker. They'd told their town friends, the Alloway sisters, and they also showed up, needles at the ready. Everyone said they were honored to help.

Clara was more relieved than she'd expected to be. And grateful. No one faulted her. In fact, they complimented her on how much she'd completed in so short a time. They'd all swooped in to help as part of a community in a time of need. She found herself talking, even laughing at times, and listening to stories of the "early days" as they bonded over something Clara was familiar with and good at—needlework. She'd felt a part of the community group and part of Persimmon Hollow. It was a new feeling for her. One she liked.

PART III

December 11, 1898

Advent, Week Three—Joy

The gold- and silver-colored embroidery on the chasuble shimmered in sunlight from the nearby window when Father O'Connell raised his arms during Mass that Sunday. How perfect, thought Clara, to see sunbeams dance in such a way on Gaudete Sunday, the Sunday of joy, of light and hope, in a season of waiting.

She felt renewed gratitude for the community that gathered to ensure the chasuble was finished in time. Father O'Connell had been speechless for a few minutes when the women gifted it to him. He'd arrived late, tired and thirsty, after saying Mass at a church many miles away. The set lines around his mouth creased into ones of surprise and then happiness when he unwrapped the paper encasing the chasuble and saw the vestment.

"God bless you, dear ladies," he said. "God bless you for everything you do."

The pleasure of the moment carried through the rest of the morning and infused Mass. The bright, sparkling light of the day prodded Clara to look into her own dark corners, to think, really think, about her plans and motives and behaviors.

After receiving Communion, she knelt and prayed anew for God's assistance. She knew she was behaving poorly and that her dissatisfaction with her new home was unbecoming. Why couldn't she accept God's will? Find and accept all that was good here? Including Billy, her heart whispered. Why couldn't she stop pushing him away, pushing away her feelings for him?

Part of her knew why. Keeping him at arm's length would make it hurt less when he learned she likely couldn't bear children. When he turned away.

Dear Lord, she prayed, *I know my stubborn streak is a mile wide and my worries are deep. I know my attitude tests my family's patience. Help me, please, dear Lord,* she prayed. *Help me find my way and put myself in your hands.*

Clara always felt peaceful and joyful after receiving the Holy Eucharist and feeling the closeness of Jesus in her heart and soul. Today was no exception. She knew God's path for her would become clear. She just didn't know how. She prayed she'd recognize it.

After the last notes of the closing hymn faded, Clara slid her glance away from the altar. As though planned, her gaze met Billy's. He sat across the aisle and a few rows forward. His face lit up. She lifted her gloved hand in a small wave and curved her lips into a welcoming smile.

Meg nudged her and gave her a knowing look. Clara ignored her and tried to look disinterested. But her heart was gladdened by the exchange of smiles.

Hours later, as the family relaxed on the porch after Sunday dinner, it dawned on Clara that the Lord's plan for her might involve Billy. The timing of their encounter at the end of Mass, right after she'd prayed so hard for guidance, could have meant something.

On the other hand, maybe she was imagining things. Better wait, she thought, before thinking she had determined God's will. She'd wait until she traveled north for the wedding. She'd see what God sent her way during that trip. It might be a sign to stay with her original plan.

As soon as she thought that, she looked at the familiar faces of her family around her and felt a deep love. Father read the paper and mother a novel. Meg and Harvey sat close together on the porch swing and held hands. Melvin stretched out on the wood floor and played with Frosty, their black dog with random white tips coloring his fur. Hattie dozed.

The slightly cool weather kissed Clara's face and the scent of citrus blossoms seemed to come right from heaven. The north seemed very distant.

Clara sensed tension in the church as she and her family arrived at Christmas choir practice. People milled around in three groups that she guessed were the Catholics, Methodists, and Baptists.

It should have been a happy occasion. Yet she saw worry creasing faces. Her breath started to constrict. It always did when she was uneasy about anything. She sat down in a pew and calmed herself with a Hail Mary.

Billy emerged from the throng and crossed the room. He greeted everyone but sat down next to Clara.

"Remember when I told you there's nothing to worry about in Persimmon Hollow as long as you were within a certain circle of people?"

Clara did remember, because his comment had been at odds with his talk of Persimmon Hollow as some kind of utopia.

"That circle is wide and covers Persimmon Hollow," he

continued. "This is a town of good people. But there are exceptions in outlying areas."

"Yes, but you have that everywhere," she said. "The city where I'm from is full of unhappy, angry people who lash out at others in hurtful, sometimes criminal ways."

"We're a lot smaller than a city," Billy said. "We were founded on values that attracted settlers interested in faith, family, and community. People who have integrity."

This was the first time Clara had seen him so uneasy. Even the alligator incident hadn't caused his brow to wrinkle as deeply. Frown lines emerged from around his pressed lips.

The church door opened again and the Sisters of St. Francis ushered in a group of children Clara assumed were from the orphanage. She saw Billy's mother draw one of the sisters aside and speak to her in low tones. Closer to where Clara sat, she overheard a woman tell another that she was sick to think anyone in their town would cause trouble.

"Sounds like you have city-type problems here," Clara said to Billy. "Who's causing such unrest?"

Billy blew out an audible breath. "They're roughnecks from outside town. They don't like anybody who doesn't look or think like them. A while ago some folks tried to mess with the school for Black children. The sisters had wanted to teach all local children together but state laws prevented that. So a separate school was built and some folks raised a fuss. People in town stood together and stopped the opposition."

Only awful people would protest education, thought Clara. That was a strike against Persimmon Hollow as a permanent home.

"Now they've gone after Lue Gim Gong," Billy said. He fisted his hands on his thighs. "That's what's got everybody so upset."

"Who?" Clara asked.

Billy explained that Lue was a Chinese immigrant who'd

come to Persimmon Hollow from the north years before with his adoptive family. Lue had quickly made a name for himself as a horticultural genius. He stayed in town after his benefactor died and willed him her land. He was known statewide and beyond.

"The reason we have any fully bearing citrus trees at the grove right now is because Lue developed a cold-hardy variety that survived that big freeze," Billy said. "They're the experimental citrus trees I told you about."

His animation returned. "The largest trees in your father's grove—the ones that bear the most fruit—are those experimental varieties Lue bred. Most people didn't grow them at first. My dad was a big believer early on. He planted a lot. Saved us when many people went under after the freeze."

That freeze again, thought Clara.

"Anyway, the troublemakers don't like Chinese people any more than they like Black people," Billy said. "Or Catholics. Jewish people are on their list, too."

A chill passed over Clara and she drew her shawl closer around her shoulders. She sought in vain to recover the peace she'd felt only days ago sitting in this very church.

"They rode through Lue's property last night," Billy said. "Broke the windows in his greenhouse. Then scared him half to death by galloping up to his door and circling around making threats."

"They should be arrested," said Clara.

"Don't know who half of them are," Billy said. "They're cowards. They cover their faces when they go around spreading hate."

Clara was unnerved. "I don't think I want to live here any longer," she said, then clamped a hand over her mouth. Billy didn't need to hear that.

"No! Clara! They're not as much of a menace as they'd like to be. We have good people here. More than enough to ward them off. Good always overcomes evil. You know that. We just have to fight hard against it. Sometimes the other side makes temporary gains."

He shifted so that he faced her and clasped one of her hands between his.

"Please don't leave," he said. "They will never come within a mile of you, I'll make sure of that. They'd have to pass through me first. And the more we stand firm, the stronger we are against all things evil. We can't give up."

She was caught in his earnest gaze. She believed him. Something about the confidence in his voice and the concern for her. And more. Something more was there. Her heart fluttered.

"The men are riding out to Lue's tomorrow to fix the greenhouse," Billy said. "After that, I'd like to bring you out there for a visit. You'd like Lue. He's a kind man, close to his animals—he has a pet rooster. He's a generous man, too generous to outsiders who don't always pay for their mail orders."

Before she could reply, Billy's mother tapped a podium and called the group to attention.

"Before we begin rehearsal, let's pray for Lue and also for his attackers," Agnes said. "Would you lead us in prayer?" she asked the sister who was clearly in charge of the orphanage group.

The praying eased Clara's tension and a sense of quietude crept back into her. By the time they closed with the Prayer to St. Michael, she spoke the words with more breath and volume than she thought possible from herself. "Be our protection against the wickedness and the snares of the devil," she recited, firm in her belief, and boosted by the conviction she heard in the voices around her.

A glimmer of joy again pushed into Clara's guarded heart. She remembered her mother's comment about how Advent was a season of hope. She still had to figure out which direction God was pointing. But inch by inch, she was opening her heart to his will.

Agnes called out the first hymn name and page number. The shuffle and ripple of paper filled the room as singers opened their hymnals. Agnes played starter notes on the portable melodeon someone had brought. Clara took a breath and wondered if she could muster up the deeper breaths needed for singing.

A half hour later, she admitted aloud what she knew in private. Singing wasn't her strength. Somehow, her short-winded efforts didn't bother her as much as they would have in the past. She liked being part of this community choir and enjoyed making the effort. But she was relieved when Agnes called a break.

"I've given it my best but I need to stop," Clara announced between long indrawn breaths that, at first, didn't provide the sustenance she needed. "Maybe I can best serve by singing only one or two songs with the group."

Her mother, sister, aunt, and several other women hurried over and ushered her to a pew amid coos and clucks and advice. She saw Billy watching her and felt comforted at his expression of concern. He looked from one woman to the next, all speaking at once to Clara. When his glance settled on her, he gave her a look that spoke of far more than choirs and songs.

Her mother scrutinized Clara's glowing expression and the direction of her gaze, looked over her shoulder, and saw Billy. She turned her face back toward Clara and then shared a glance with Billy's mother. Agnes returned an unspoken nod of some kind of agreement.

Dismay tugged at Clara. Would her family forever treat her as a youngster around whom they couldn't speak freely? She was twenty-two. Her own mother was married with a baby on the way at that age.

The short break over, practice resumed. Clara picked up her latest embroidery project and moved closer to one of the dim electric lights used sparingly at church to keep down costs. The lights covered the room with a warm glow.

The daisy motif she stitched along the edge of a dishtowel didn't require as much attention as the chasuble had. Thoughts raced through her mind. Her heart was dangerously close to falling all the way for Billy. He'd attracted her from the start and the feeling had deepened after she began to know him—his good heart, quick intelligence, bold dreams. He treated her as an equal, as though her infirmities were simply a part of her to accept with the whole, not something that set her apart. He treated her gently but as a desirable woman.

She wished he'd consider a future beyond Persimmon Hollow. She wondered if it would be too much to ask of him. His life was here, she knew. His entire family was here. Most of hers was, too. His plans were here. His love of the land was here.

She tried to imagine him confined by city streets. The picture wouldn't form. She tried to imagine herself as a homestead wife. That image wouldn't form, either. The vision that emerged was one of her strolling through an art museum.

That made her think of one of her favorite paintings, one she'd seen only in a book and that had touched her soul: *Christ in the Wilderness*. She could almost feel Christ wrestling with his emotions and the struggles of those long days in the desert. Sometimes she felt she lived in a desert that restricted her movements and left her unable to reach beyond a tiny protective circle. She wished for Christ's strength.

"Hattie, a bit softer if you're able," Agnes called above the crowd to Aunt Hattie, whose voice had been drowning out several others. "Let the others help round out your unique style."

Unique. Yes, she and Hattie certainly were the different ones, thought Clara. Was Aunt Hattie, her primary hope for a return to the familiar, going to stay here? If yes, was that also some kind of message? Clara wondered if she should let the people in Persimmon Hollow help round her into someone who fit in this alien land.

So many questions. She lowered her gaze to the fabric and

resumed a gentle, rhythmic stitching. Needle and thread and the soft feel of fabric in her hands always settled calmness on her.

Except tonight. She hated not having the threads of her life neatly knotted and flowing smoothly. Flowing in the direction she chose, she admitted. Life was already challenging for her. Now, with Billy and the others here, it had become more complex. She pushed her needle through the hooped fabric with more force than usual and pricked her finger. Around her, the choir sang.

True to his offer, Billy arranged a visit to the horticulturist later that week. The weather had broken, he and other old-timers told Clara.

"Couldn't ask for a better day than this!" Billy said as they reached Lue's property. "This is normal mid-December weather." He helped Clara out of the cart while Harvey did the same for Meg. Aunt Hattie, who'd invited herself, was already out and stretching her legs.

Clara had to agree the air felt delicious, not too cold, not too hot, just as perfect as one could ask for. Wrens, mockingbirds, cardinals, and towhees chirped and sang as though they agreed. The sunlight brightened her mood instead of stifling her. A gentle breeze carried a hint of coolness.

"It'd be wonderful if it were like this year-round," she said.

"No such luck," Billy answered. "But we do have a few months when my gratitude for living here soars beyond the usual bounds. You'll see. Give it a year."

Clara didn't answer. The small group approached the house and yard where a slender man with a rooster on his shoulder petted a horse who nuzzled his arm. Other visitors milled around and grove workers tended the largest citrus trees Clara had yet seen.

Lue bowed and welcomed them and thanked Billy and Harvey for their help with the greenhouse repair. He was not much taller than she was, Clara saw. She immediately sensed an innate gentleness and kindness in him and felt at ease.

"Soon I'll have some fern that's better adapted for this climate," he said to Billy. "Come, I'll show you." He led the way into the greenhouse and over to a section dominated by small pots containing wispy growth of a springlike green color.

"Already?" Billy was excited. He and Lue inspected the young fronds and Billy turned to Clara. "I had a bunch of fern slips mailed here to launch my fernery," he told her. "The property I'm buying is right next to Lue's. I'll show you when we leave here. No, wait, I've got to get back to the grove. Tomorrow, okay? We planted a small test plot and the ferns are already doing better than expected. Others are growing in the greenhouse here. Lue is breeding new varieties with better tolerance to different weather conditions. His ferns will be a win atop a win."

Billy's passion for the fernery project infected even Clara along with everyone else. She actually wanted to see what a fernery looked like. Harvey questioned Billy and Lue about citrus and fern cultivation. Hattie sought Billy's input on fernery pricing, long-term projections, and land costs. Clara noticed how Billy answered each question like the pro he was. He'd obviously studied long and deep about the subject.

After a while, Clara wandered off to inspect the other plants. She was only steps away when she overheard Billy and Lue explain to Harvey how fern needed protection from Florida's occasional hard freezes. She frowned. Such tender fern would never survive a northern winter. Neither would Billy. He'd wither if pulled from his Florida roots.

Her conscience tugged at her wavering inflexibility about life in Persimmon Hollow. Day by day, slim but strong tendrils grabbed ahold of the slender pillars she admitted to finding—and liking—in her new home. Like Billy, of course. But also like the smell of the citrus blossoms on the small trees growing in urns she stood in front of at the moment. The trees contained maturing lemons along with blooming flowers whose scent was straight from heaven. There was no other way to describe the aroma.

Clara closed her eyes and acknowledged her new feelings. With them came a newfound joy in herself and in life.

Why not stay where she was planted? Her stubbornness tugged, unwilling to give up too easily. She'd made a plan to return. Clara hated changing a good plan. Her world functioned best when planned, organized, and predictable. Florida was anything but.

Plus, her museum project was up north, not here. She hadn't heard anything from friends about the plans she'd put in their hands when she moved. Her long, detailed notes and outlines. The ones she'd spent so much time developing. The historical society hadn't contacted her, either. Why not? They had received support from the community—pledges and offers of antique furniture and other treasures for display. Was it all for naught?

Yes, it was still only a germ of an idea, but one she had loved being involved with. Even better, her role in it was something she was physically able to pursue.

The rustling from Meg's dress neared her.

"Look out, Aunt Hattie is as interested as Harvey," Meg said. "She's calculating investment opportunities and land purchases."

"That doesn't mean she wants to live here year-round," Clara replied.

"You'll never uproot Billy from this place, you know that," Meg said. "And if Aunt Hattie gets sand in her shoes, as the locals say, she'll move here in a heartbeat. Your relocation scheme will fall apart. I won't be sorry if it does. Neither will your new beau."

Clara put her hands on her hips and blew out a breath. "I don't know what you're talking about."

"Stop lying to yourself," Meg said.

Clara turned to face her annoying older sister. A retort was forming when the rest of the party caught up with them, faces aglow with excitement. Clara's irritation faded in the face of their cheerfulness. She clamped her lips closed. She hated when Meg was right.

The tingly air on her face made Clara halt in wonder as she stepped out of the house and looked around. Overnight, the weather had turned cold. Icy if you judged by the locals. The workers helping her father in the grove were bundled in layers of clothing, with knit caps drawn close over their heads and ears. They took frequent breaks around the burn barrel and exclaimed about how cold it was for midday.

The temperature was in the low fifties but seemed colder. Clara had donned her cloak and gloves. She wriggled her fingers inside her gloves and adjusted her scarf. Despite the chill, it was a crisp, sunny, beautiful day for an outing to Billy's fern property.

Meg skipped the excursion to help their mother with chores but Aunt Hattie and Harvey were already off the porch and waiting for Billy to arrive.

"Come, Clara," Aunt Hattie called to her. "Let's walk out to the street and wait there." Harvey was already a few steps ahead.

She joined them and smelled the sharp, crisp air. The trio reached the street just as Billy's wagon rattled toward them.

Clara laughed aloud. She could hardly see him underneath his winter clothes, atop which he'd wrapped himself in a quilt. Even the horse wore a blanket.

"Hey, no fair," he called as he stopped. "I know why you're laughing. But it almost never stays this cold during the middle of the day. It's not even in the mid-fifties. I hope we don't get a freeze tonight."

Clara sobered. If there was one thing she'd learned about Florida, it was how damaging a freeze could be.

"Do you expect one?" she asked as he helped her to the carriage seat. Hattie refused help and scrambled in after her. Harvey climbed into the back.

"Not from what I've read from the wind and clouds," Billy said. "But nature is unpredictable. We'll hope and pray for the best but be ready for the worst."

She nodded. She noticed how her silk-lined wool cloak and leather gloves contrasted with the worn boards of the wagon's plank seat and floor. What a snobbish thought, she told herself. She instantly felt humbled. The simplicity and earthiness of her surroundings, in cart and out, framed and emphasized what was really important: the man she sat next to, the aunt on her other side, the almost-brother-in-law in the back.

Somehow, the setting—so stripped down to essentials—made the value of human connection all the more visible. An inner warmth flowed through her. Clara glanced upward and offered a silent whisper of thanks to the Blessed Virgin, for she suspected that the awareness and gentle nudge had come from her.

One tenacious part of Clara remained unyielding, though. Her companions took their good health for granted. She sometimes wished others could view the world through her eyes. Maybe then, they'd understand that her hesitation about embracing new things and places rested a great deal in her fears about her abilities. With the familiar, she knew exactly where and how she could function.

Clara thought about the activities open to her in Persimmon Hollow: needlework, visits, walks, concerts and theatricals, canoe trips…Canoe trips? Memories of the excursion bubbled up. Funny, the joyful memories of that morning far outweighed ones of the alligator encounter.

She glanced at Billy, then quickly looked away. Stop it right there, Clara, she told herself. Stop falling in love with Billy.

"Is there really a literary society in town?" she asked, seemingly out of the blue. She wanted to chase away the other images pushing into her thoughts, images dominated by a future with Billy.

"Huh, oh, yeah, but it's based at the college, not in town," Billy said. "My sister can tell you more about it. It's like a book club. You might like it and they'd welcome a new member. They don't meet during Advent but will start up again after the New Year."

Great. That's when she should be finalizing her departure. Should be? No, would be. Was her certainty slipping more than she was willing to acknowledge?

"Tell me more about investment in ferneries," Hattie asked. "I've a good mind to start one myself."

"That'd be great!" Billy enthused. "We'd have the beginnings of a fern cooperative."

"I like the idea already," Hattie said. "Working together benefits everyone."

"We're going to need a cooperative," Billy said. "The fern market is getting ready to explode. Florists already use the greenery in bouquets and I read that people are showcasing ferns as part of their home decorations."

"I better get busy!" Hattie enthused.

Clara frowned and pulled her hood tighter after a cold breeze chilled her neck. Yes, she'd be planning her departure, maybe. Assuming Aunt Hattie wasn't set on planning one in the other direction. Assuming the doubts growing inside her didn't multiply.

Clara wondered again why she couldn't just accept her situation and make the best of it. That's what she counseled anyone who asked how she coped with ill health. She said she lived with it and made do. Which she surely wasn't doing right now. Not when she gripped to the plan formed hastily during her earliest days in Persimmon Hollow.

The cart turned onto a narrow lane adjacent to Lue's property and rocked along an uneven, sandy path through an oak-canopied piece of land. Sunlight filtered through the tall treetops. The level ground was open between the trees except for low growth and the fenced-off test plot.

"It's like being in an outdoor cathedral," Clara murmured.

Billy impulsively grabbed her hand and squeezed it gently. "I feel God here and in so many places when I work outdoors."

Time seemed to slow in the shady confines of the property. The four of them walked a leisurely pace despite the chill. Clara studied Billy as he, Hattie, and Harvey clustered around the test plot and inspected the fern foliage, roots, soil, and patterns of sunlight. Her heart squeezed. She was so drawn to him. Was it because he was so different than she was? Outdoorsy and bold and strong compared to her quietness and frailty? No, it was more. He understood her. Respected her. She knew she'd never fear anything with him by her side.

By her side is where she wanted him at that very moment. She had such an urge to feel his arms around her and his lips on hers. The strength of the feeling surprised her.

Clara turned away to settle her quickened breath. She walked over to where a stronger beam of sunlight drifted through the oak leaves like an angel's rays. Footsteps followed and she turned to see Billy next to her.

"Can you imagine a house here?" he asked. "I always thought I'd want to build on my family's land. There's enough room and everybody's there. But something about this patch of earth makes me wonder if this isn't the place."

Clara glanced up at him. "What kind of house? It would have to be something fitting for this beautiful setting."

He grinned. "Absolutely. A log cabin, for sure. Made from sturdy heart pine. That wood will last forever."

He glanced at her face.

"But a really nice one," he hastened to add. "Like Mom and Dad's, maybe bigger. A place my wife would love. With plenty of room for a lot of kids."

Clara thought her heart actually skipped a few beats. She closed her eyes for a long moment. Of course a man like Billy would want to father a lot of children. Her flights of fancy were getting in the way of reality. What was she thinking, that she'd stay here because they might have some kind of future together? When her doctors back home had insisted she was too frail to withstand pregnancy and childbirth?

She opened her eyes and saw Billy watching her with an expectant expression, as though waiting for her reply.

Tell him, her inner voice cried. Tell him your fears and feelings.

"I'm sure your wife would love everything about that picture," she said instead. She hoped she'd kept her voice neutral. She didn't smile and wouldn't look Billy in the eye.

She half-turned away from him but glanced up sideways through her lashes, so he wouldn't notice.

His enthusiasm had dimmed and his eager smile had vanished.

"We'd best get back to the others," he said.

She gave a small nod. The sun had shifted away from them. The day felt cold again.

"Where's the bank in this town?" Aunt Hattie asked the next morning at breakfast. "I need to transfer funds. Looks like I'm making this move permanent. The new fern industry and the land opportunities are too good to overlook. And my bones creak less here."

Clara gulped the mouthful of coffee she'd just sipped. Her

cup rattled more than usual as she set it down. She glanced at Meg, who widened her eyes in return. They both looked at their mother, whose placid face showed a faint line radiating from her slightly compressed lips.

"Clara will walk downtown and show me," Aunt Hattie commanded as she dabbed her lips with her napkin and rose. "We leave in half an hour."

"We'll get her situated in her own place in no time," Orville told Gertrude after Hattie left the room.

Gertrude nodded. "I do love her but she can be—"

"Trying at times," finished Clara.

"Like you," added Meg, and grinned in response to Clara's grimace.

Their father's eyes held a hint of humor. "I know how my sister can fill a room. Not to worry, she seems intent on carving her own way. She sees this as new territory to master. If nothing else, she'll keep us from becoming complacent."

He, too, rose. "The grove awaits."

Melvin followed his lead. "The store calls."

The two men departed to start their work days.

"Either of you want to join me and Aunt Hattie?" Clara asked.

"It's wash day," her mother said, and directed a meaningful look toward her. "Would you prefer to join me, Meg, and the women we hired to help with the chore?"

Clara knew her gaze showed guilt. She wasn't above using her breathing limitations to avoid that cumbersome task. And she knew her mother knew that.

"I'll help iron later," she said in a small voice.

"Excellent," said her mother as Hattie's footsteps clicked on the wooden stairs as she returned from getting ready.

"Clara, let's go."

"Coming," Clara said, and took her last gulp of coffee. "Let me get my cloak."

"This town is young, to be sure, but unique and intriguing," Hattie commented as the two strolled the few blocks to the heart of town. "I like being in on something so new."

"It's certainly different," Clara said.

"But unlikeable to you? That's why you want to live permanently with me up north?" Hattie asked. "Yes, I got your letter. A neighbor is forwarding my mail here. Sorry to disappoint you, but I'm returning north only to pack up and move south. Come to think, I'm not sorry. You need to broaden your horizons and stop focusing inward all the time."

Clara sighed. "Aunt Hattie, that's easy to you to say but—"

"… but you have fewer physical abilities than able-bodied pioneers with robust constitutions and hefty lungs," Hattie interrupted. "Yes, I know your song, my dear. I'm not unsympathetic. You have limitations. You also sometimes use them as crutches."

"I don't."

"Hmph."

They dropped the impasse when they reached First Bank of Persimmon Hollow and entered the cool, polished interior. Clara only half listened as Hattie conducted her business but perked up when she heard her name.

"Yes, open an account for Miss Clara DeForest and deposit $100."

"Aunt Hattie!"

Her aunt turned innocent eyes toward her. "You'll need seed money if you're to launch a museum. You think I'm unaware that you miss that project from back north? So do something here. Start one here. It's something this town needs, I might add."

Clara's heart raced so much at the surprise that her breath quickened and she had to sit down. She made her way to a chair against the window wall and sank down into it before she went light-headed. Yes, she dearly missed her museum work. The idea of launching something here, though, was daunting. The youthful town lacked resources needed to support the idea. What would she even focus a collection on? The town wasn't old enough to have a history.

"If anyone's up to such a task, you are, my dear," her aunt said as she followed her over and took the adjacent seat. "Just take small steps, as you are able. And always pray for guidance."

Two women entered the bank with heads bowed together. They talked in rapid, hushed tones and were unaware that Clara and Hattie sat nearby.

"Another attack? Are you certain?" one woman asked the other.

"Yes, the men from the Knights of Columbus somehow found out and got there just in time to stop them from causing damage," the second woman said. "They were aiming for the experimental part of his nursery. From what I understand, they had enough kerosene to start a serious fire. Were starting to pour it near the foundation of his house."

"No!" the first woman said. "That poor man. And all because he's a different race."

"Yes, I was almost sick to my stomach when I heard. And I only heard because the men were talking outside when they returned and didn't know I was outdoors. I'd gone out to check on the chickens. The men shut up in a heartbeat soon as I came around the side of the house. I don't know any other details."

"There must be something we can do."

"But what?"

"I'll tell you what!" Hattie was out of her chair. Her heels clicked as she crossed the few feet that separated her and Clara from the two women.

"I know you're of my faith because I heard you mention the Knights," Hattie continued. "I'm new here. Hattie DeForest."

The two women nodded and introduced themselves.

"The men should start nightly patrols and we women will commit to providing coffee and other nourishment they'll need,"

Hattie continued. "We should also launch some kind of women's group to discuss more permanent solutions. No one should have to live in fear of such atrocities."

"The men won't take kindly to us deciding on their actions," the first woman said. "And I'd be surprised if they weren't already keeping a close eye on things."

"We could certainly discuss the other idea, a women's group," the second said. "Although any action we might take could raise the ire of the troublemakers. If we're correct in our assumptions, these folks don't like people of our faith."

"That's too bad," Hattie said. "Because we're not going anywhere."

You, maybe, thought Clara, who'd listened to every word. She wanted to huddle in a corner until she could transport herself to a more civilized place.

Christmas was little more than a week away. Her trip started the day after that. She was running out of time to solidify her next steps.

Christmas. She bemoaned her lack of seasonal spirit. She fretted she wouldn't finish the gifts she was making. She had trouble sustaining joyful holiday feelings even when they did emerge, like during Gaudete Sunday. She wished she could drag them back.

It's Advent, she reminded herself, a season of hope and waiting for light. She almost laughed. Light was something Persimmon Hollow had in abundance. She'd do well to embrace it. So what if there was no snow. Holiday baking would soon ramp up. Scents of cinnamon, nutmeg, and ginger would boost her spirits. They always did.

She looked down at her hands placed one atop the other in her lap, the way she'd been taught to do when out in society— the way that didn't matter here, from what she'd observed. And so what, an inner voice prodded. Clouds shifted outside and sunlight poured through the window behind her, warming her inside and out.

Hattie dominated the three-way conversation with the two strangers until a bank clerk intervened and asked about the incoming women's financial concerns. Hattie clomped back over to Clara, eyes ablaze.

"Well, I never! I'm incensed beyond words," Hattie proclaimed as she and Clara started making their way back home. "I've a mind to confront those men myself but the women said that would be foolhardy. Said the culprits would enjoy showing their brand of justice to an outsider such as myself."

Hattie launched into a tangent about why an armed woman could stand up to anyone. Clara only half-listened. Aunt Hattie was sometimes too bold for her own good. A confrontation in this frontier land could well result in Hattie's injury or even death.

Clara knew her family would hear all about the bank encounter and Hattie's plans before the day ended. She wanted the counsel of someone who knew Persimmon Hollow better than her family did. We're still newcomers, she thought. Her disabilities had taught her how to assess and read places and situations to determine how best to maneuver within them. Her heightened senses told her Hattie needed to step carefully and with forethought and on a less hostile course. Who could help her figure that out?

The question had barely flitted through her mind before the answer followed. Billy would know what to do. She needed to get word to him, right away. Before Hattie did something rash. Judging by the fiery rhetoric of the woman beside her, that left little time.

Clara fretted over the town's limited telephone service. How could she quickly get word to Taylor Grove? She remembered seeing a hand-cranked telephone mounted on the wall the day she and Meg visited the Taylors.

Clara turned and started walking in the other direction.

"Where are we going?" Hattie asked.

"To the furniture store," Clara said. "They have a telephone and I want to contact Taylor Grove right away. We need to call a community meeting, soon."

"No arguments from me on that," Hattie said.

No one answered the operator's repeated rings to the Taylors' phone. After Clara and Hattie relayed the bank conversation to Clara's brother, he jumped into action. "I'll ride out there," Melvin said. "I'll stop at the house first. Will you mind the store until Harvey or Dad can get here?"

Clara and Hattie settled down as much as they could. The store was quiet. Together they said a rosary until Harvey raced in and they were free to leave.

"First, we stage a protest march," Hattie said to the gathering assembled in the DeForest living room the next evening.

"This is a town, not a city," said Seth Taylor. He and Agnes and their adult children Billy and Polly filled the room with Clara and her parents, siblings, aunt, and Harvey.

"Plus, it's almost Christmas," Agnes added.

"Who would you convince with a protest march?" Seth asked. "Everybody already knows what's going on. You'll annoy the ones who hate. They'll react the way a wounded alligator would. We'd have bloodshed."

"Your family has the deepest roots here," Orville DeForest said to Seth. "What do you suggest?"

Clara stood off to one side, ironing the dress collars, cuffs and aprons that hadn't been finished on wash day. Billy had nudged Melvin away from Clara and took over his job of rotating the flat irons atop a closed wood heater. As the iron

Clara used cooled, Billy switched it out with a hot one and put the cold one back on the stove to reheat.

He was attentive but subdued. Clara hoped it was because of the seriousness of the topic and not because of their conversation at the fernery property. She needed to let him know, soon, the full extent of her disabilities. She needed him to understand why she kept ahold of the idea of leaving Persimmon Hollow. Of leaving him.

Seth pressed his lips together as he considered Orville's question. Clara had learned earlier how Seth had lived here since before the town was founded. That he'd faced his own troubles years before.

"Open displays of firmness without rancor," Seth said. "There are more of us in town than the troublemakers from neighboring areas. We'll provide quiet but visible support."

"Bah! I say fight," Hattie said.

"An eye for an eye makes everyone blind," said Agnes, who sat on the settee, fingering her rosary. "Besides, they wouldn't fight back against us. They'd double their hatred toward their targets."

"Agnes is right," Seth said. "We'll do what we can. The town militia that formed earlier this year never disbanded. There were far more volunteers than President McKinley needed to fight in Cuba, so the government asked residents to be vigilant on the home front. Not that we expected to find Spanish ships on the river in this part of the state, but you never know. We stopped patrolling when the war ended but we didn't disband. I'll call on everyone. Our group has black, white and brown members. We'll make sure outsiders steer clear of Lue's property and Persimmon Hollow as a whole. I'm not too worried. They know we're a force to be reckoned with. It's a shame we can't stop these groups everywhere in the state. That requires backbone from lawmakers who—"

"Who need to give women the vote!" Hattie interrupted. "These problems would end if only women had their say."

Clara coughed. Hattie would vote for blood and guts. Meg sat forward in her chair and nudged the leg of the ironing board with her foot. Clara looked up. *Change the conversation, quick!* Meg mouthed to Clara.

"Hattie, you also mentioned hoping to start a women's group," Clara said.

"A women's group?" Gertrude asked. Agnes also turned toward Hattie.

"Yes, to fundraise and find other ways to support the effort," Hattie said. "Women must do their part."

"Perhaps after you get settled here," Gertrude suggested. "We could meet to discuss the idea."

"I'll organize something after the holidays," Agnes said.

Billy turned toward Clara. "I'd be happy to carry you anywhere you need to go, until we're sure there won't be any more trouble. Just to be on the safe side."

"Oh, Billy, I couldn't disrupt your life like that," she said automatically.

Disappointment flitted across Billy's face. He busied himself with the flat irons, lining them in precise order and holding his hand near their bases to gauge heat levels. Clara yearned for him to turn her way with one of his trademark smiles and tell her it wouldn't be a disruption, that he'd be honored to drive her around. To answer the way he'd been doing since they met.

A sizzle escaped the fabric she ironed. Clara jerked the iron back. She'd scorched a sleeve cuff.

"Everybody's tired," Gertrude announced, and rose from her chair.

Agnes followed her example and got up. "Agreed. I'm sure Lupita is ready to hand the little ones back to me and Seth. We can't solve anything in one discussion, but we've made a start."

"We'll pray for hope and healing this Sunday—and every Sunday," Gertrude said. "Every day, in fact."

"Amen," said Agnes.

"To end the evening on a lighter note, everyone's invited to join our Christmas tree-cutting expedition next week," Polly said as the Taylor clan gathered their things and made ready to leave.

Clara glanced up and caught Billy looking at her. "It's a long day, but a lot of fun," he said.

All her private declarations about keeping her distance flew away when she met his gaze. "I'd love to go," she said. "It sounds new and exciting." *Had she really just said that?*

"Great, we'll count you in," he said.

The joy that had drained from Clara earlier seeped back when Billy took her hands in his. "I'm looking forward to it," he said, and gave her hands a light squeeze that she returned. She resisted the urge to stand up on her toes and kiss him lightly on the lips. Instead, she let her happiness shine through her eyes and smile. "Me, too." She walked with him to the door.

The Taylors departed with hearty goodbyes and hand waves. Clara closed the door behind them and turned to see Meg standing there, arms crossed.

"It's true, there's hope for you yet," Meg said, and grinned and scooted away before Clara could grab her.

"Merry Christmas to you, too," Clara called after her sister.

But nobody was more surprised than she was at how happy she felt.

PART IV

Advent, Week Four—Love

Clara gripped the pastry bag and applied a thin, even line of icing just inside the edge of each tree-shaped cookie on the tray. She traded the bag with green icing for one with white, and started adding tiny dots to mimic candlelight.

At the other end of the kitchen table, her mother rolled out dough for pie crusts. Meg stood at the stove, stirring and then removing from the heat a pot of dried apples she had been reconstituting. Aunt Hattie stood by the dry sink, greasing and flouring pie tins.

Scents of cinnamon, apples, cloves, vanilla, and pumpkin mingled and drifted on the air, carried by the gentle breeze through the open windows. The weather was superb. Another stellar Persimmon Hollow day, is how Billy would describe it, Clara thought.

She set down the pastry bag, flexed and unflexed her fingers and raised and lowered her shoulders to alleviate the stiffness from her exertions.

"Your decorating is so beautiful!" Meg said, as she removed fruitcakes from the pie safe and brought them to the table. "Not a speck out of place. If I did it, the icing would be dripping off the edges of the cookies."

"That's why Clara has the job," their mother said, and all four of them laughed.

Clara wished her life was as tidy as her cookie icing. Yet, at this moment, she felt calm and at peace, warm and loving toward everyone and everything. She'd finally embraced the Christmas spirit. She felt good and, dare she say it even to herself, at home.

The thought of the upcoming wedding trip sparked another spurt of joy in her. *Thank you God*, she prayed silently, *for everything and for putting up with my ungratefulness of late.*

Her mother brushed the table clear of crumbs and Meg set down the fruitcakes. Hattie handed Gertrude the pie tins. Clara eyed the table. Between the cookies and fruitcakes, she, Meg, and Hattie had a fair amount of wrapping to do while Gertrude focused on the pies.

"Better get started," her mother said as she started to position pie dough into the round tins. "We need to be finished before hungry men arrive looking for a hot meal."

Clara wrapped as neatly as she decorated. She creased and folded parchment paper and wrapped each fruitcake in a neat package.

"Clara, are you going to share any details about your plan for permanently leaving Persimmon Hollow?" her mother asked, as though she were discussing the weather. "Yes, I did catch the comment Meg made on the porch days ago. Of course I asked Hattie and Meg about it since you weren't forthcoming."

Clara's hand slipped on the rectangle of paper she was folding.

"And we need details about your courtship with Billy," added Meg.

"We're not courting," Clara said, too quickly.

"Sure you're not," said Meg, and released an exaggerated sigh. "All handsome young outdoorsmen hang around after dropping off their mothers to sew here. And pretend to be interested in a vestment a bunch of women are embroidering. What was his excuse again, for lingering that day? Oh, yes, he felt a duty to learn more in case he ever needs to pick up thread for his mother again at the store. Please. Why, just the other night he offered to drive you around anytime and anyplace. That's more than being neighborly."

"I agree with your sister," Gertrude said. "He didn't invite anyone but you for a walk when we took a break from the embroidery. Your happiness was evident when you returned and it lasted long after everyone left. I've also noticed you've become quite interested in ferns recently."

"Such a nice young man," interspersed Hattie. "Helpful and generous with his fern knowledge without expecting anything in return. Says a lot about his character."

"Okay, I'll talk—about the idea of moving," Clara said. She wanted—needed—to unburden her thoughts.

"Mother, yes, I thought to return to live permanently in our old town," she said. "I was going to ask your and Dad's permission to move in with Aunt Hattie after the holiday season."

"My relocation squashes that idea," Hattie said. "Her plan has a residence snag."

"And a Billy snag," Meg added.

The crinkle of parchment paper and soft thud of the rolling pin were the only sounds for the next few minutes.

"You're still unhappy here?" Gertrude asked.

Clara searched her heart. Was she? "I thought so, or did until a short while ago," she said. She reiterated the reasons that had jelled: how everyone's robust heartiness made her feel out of place; the town's rough-edged social graces; the physical smal-less of Persimmon Hollow; the lack of refined activities; her sadness about leaving her museum project. Somehow they didn't seem as important as they once did.

When she stopped talking, the other three waited as though she weren't finished.

Her heart beat a little faster.

"And, as much as I like—more than like—Billy Taylor, I'm a city girl and he's a country boy through and through."

Gertrude set aside her rolling pin. Hattie and Meg stopped tying ribbons around the fruitcakes Clara had packaged. Clara had their undivided attention.

"He's a country boy who deserves a healthy wife who can bear children," she said. Her voice was small. She angrily blinked back tears before anyone else saw them.

There. She'd finally spoken the words aloud.

Her mother moved to stand behind her. She leaned in and wrapped her arms around Clara.

"God allows love to bloom in ways only He understands," she said.

"I know," Clara whispered, and squeezed her mother's arms.

"You ought to let Billy decide what he thinks on the matter," Meg piped up. "Besides, maybe you can have a little one some-day. Don't give up hope. Medical science is advancing all the time. And you're getting stronger the longer you live here. It's obvious."

"Very true," their mother added.

"Want me to ask Billy for you?" Hattie said. "You know me, no subject is off limits."

Clara straightened and her mother removed her arms and returned to the other side of the table.

"Aunt Hattie, don't you dare," Clara said. "Besides, I already know what he thinks."

Again, the three women looked at her.

She told them what he'd said the day they'd looked over his fern property, about building a house large enough for a lot of children.

"I've never spoken to him specifically about having or not having children, but he knows the basics about my health condition," she added, into the silence that had sucked some of the holiday cheer out of the kitchen. "Even if, by some miracle, I can carry a baby to term and give birth, I can't imagine being strong enough to have several."

"Well, my advice is to clear the air with Billy, and don't wait to do so," Hattie said.

"For once your aunt and I agree," Gertrude added. "Now let's get this wrapping finished and pies in the oven. Nothing like work to focus the mind and move it away from our problems."

Clara tried but couldn't fully nudge her problems out of the way. She made a decision as she started to assemble Christmas gift packages of decorated cookies. She might be physically frail but she'd been acting like a moral coward, too. For that, there was no excuse. She would be forthright with Billy about everything. He deserved that. She'd do it before she left in—she gulped—six days. In less than a week, she'd be on the train heading north. And possibly only coming back to say goodbye again.

"It's quite a caravan," Clara said to Billy. She clung to the wagon's side railing as the cart lurched through the sugary sand ruts in what Billy called the Big Scrub. A chattering group of orphans in the wagon bed talked, laughed, and shouted every time they saw a bird or imagined they saw a bear.

She shared their excitement. She hadn't expected an outing to cut down a Christmas tree in Florida to be so much fun. Even her nostalgia for tall firs from the woods back home receded as she gazed at the unique beauty of the landscape around her.

Behind their wagon streamed several others filled with family and friends from Taylor Grove, the orphanage, and the DeForest grove and business. The ferry had to make three trips to get everyone across the river.

"When we go this far out of town it's good to have a group in case someone's wheel falls off or something," Billy said. Clara's eyes widened. She hadn't considered the possibility of mishaps. She didn't know they'd venture so far from what passed for civilization, just to find suitable trees. But she had to admit the expedition-like atmosphere added to the fun.

"The best Christmas trees are out here in the scrub," he continued, speaking both to Clara and the youngsters. "See how the trees and shrubs are different out here?" He pointed to various greenery.

Clara couldn't really discern the varieties of plant life but she was able to register how the shrubs and trees were interspersed with patches of lichens and almost pure white sand.

Billy launched into an explanation about why the pine trees in this part of the forest—trees he called sand pines—were better suited for holiday decorating than the longleaf pines that grew all around Persimmon Hollow and Taylor Grove.

"You'll see as soon as we cut down some good ones," he finished. "They're smaller and thicker and good for decorations. Longleaf pines have their full growth way at the top."

He rolled the wagon to a stop at the bottom of a white sand hill dotted with the stubby pine trees, shrubby oaks, rounded plants that looked like the herb rosemary, lichen growth, and a thick sandy path upwards. The orphans scrambled out, the other wagons pulled in, and soon everyone was talking at once and starting off in different directions.

Clara eyed the incline as Billy helped her out. She said a quick prayer but knew she was asking for the impossible. She saw how others were already sinking and shifting their balance as they waded through the thick sand on the uphill climb. The exertion coupled with the midday warmth didn't bode well for her.

"I might wait down here," she said to Billy, as the children ran off in response to Seth Taylor's call.

"We'll take our time," Billy said. "Here, give me your hand."

She hesitated, then placed her smaller hand into his larger one. It was as though his touch sent strength through her.

"I'll do my best," she said.

"That's all I'd ever ask from you," Billy said. They hadn't started up the hill yet. Everyone else's voices started to fade as groups of tree hunters broke off in different directions.

Bill drew in a breath and turned Clara to face him. He took her other hand, so that both hers were clasped between his.

"I have to speak my mind, Clara, and I don't know when we'll be alone again. I—I—care for you. A lot. More than I ever have for any woman. I guess I'm asking if you'd consider…if it'd be okay for me to call on you as a beau. To court you. If you'd be willing to see what the future might hold for us."

He was quiet for a moment. "Because I already know what I hope that future will be," he added.

Clara stared into his eyes, which had grown darker brown as he spoke. She felt such a pull, such a tug toward him. Her heart ached and it had nothing to do with her health. She leaned toward him and laid her head against his shoulder. He instantly released her hands and put his arms around her.

"I feel your heartbeat," he said in a low voice. "Is it telling me 'yes'?"

She leaned outward and looked up at him. "Yes," she said. "And no."

Her last two words dashed some of the hope that had leapt into Billy's face.

No excuses, Clara. Spell everything out, she ordered herself.

She gazed up at the ocean-blue sky, smelled the woodsy aroma of pine, heard cardinals and mockingbirds chirp, and saw a bright blue and white Florida scrub jay alight in a shrub in the near distance.

"I care about you more than I wanted to," she said.

He released her, stepped back and half frowned. "That doesn't sound promising."

She had to smile. "That came out wrong. I care about you, Billy, a lot."

"But?"

Now it was her turn to inhale. "I may be moving back north permanently."

"But why? I thought your parents and everyone liked it here. The store's doing great and so is your grove."

"No, not my family. Me."

"But why?" he repeated.

She listed all the same reasons she'd told her family except the biggest one. Saying them aloud made them sound less important, just as they had the other day. Some of them even sounded selfish. But she'd spoken this much and was determined to finish.

"So, you see," she continued, "when I go up north for the wedding the day after Christmas, I plan to check on possible living arrangements. I was going to move in with Aunt Hattie up there, but you know what happened to that idea. She's delighted about moving here. Everything is really unsettled right now."

"I hope you don't mind me saying I hope you don't find new living arrangements," Billy said. "That you have to come back and stay. That you want to come back. Do you really dislike it that much here?"

Clara thought about the question, really thought.

"Not as much as when I first got here."

"Well, that's a start."

"A big reason for that is you," she blurted.

A hint of Billy's sunny nature crept back in to his face.

"I'm not one to back away from difficulties," he said. "I'll go up against your old city life any day. Try me. At least give me a chance. I haven't finished showing you all the great things about Persimmon Hollow. We've hardly started. Not only that, we need a museum like the one you were working on up there. Start one here. I'll help, if you'll let me."

She placed a hand on his chest and he covered it with one of his.

"There's something else, something more important than city versus country, or museums, or just about anything," she said. She couldn't meet his eyes.

He waited for her to continue.

"Billy, you need to know this about me," she said, almost stumbling over her words. "My health is worse that it might appear."

"You don't have consumption, do you?" Worry spread across his face.

"No, thank God. But I've always been told I'm not strong enough to have children. I probably can't bear children. My lungs, they're not strong enough to withstand the rigors."

Finally. Her deepest worry was loud and clear and in the open.

She heard a short intake of breath from Billy, but he masked any surprise he might have felt at her words.

"So, what's wrong with that?" he finally asked.

She peered up at him. "Do you realize what you're saying? If we continue on this path and it leads to a future together, you might never see a little Billy running around or have a daughter that looked like me or you, or…"

She watched the slightest shadow drift across his eyes as the meaning of her words sunk into him.

"Those children that you want to build a house for, out on your land, might never arrive."

His smile was gone, replaced by a look of mixed confusion, understanding, and sympathy.

"We'll adopt," he said. "I live next door to an orphanage. I was adopted by my Uncle Seth. Polly is adopted. Who knows, maybe you'll get better. We could have a big, blended family."

But Clara could see questions in his eyes.

"Stop," she whispered. "Please, don't say anything else now. It's okay. I understand. I've had to understand all my life. You don't need to cover up feelings. I care about you, Billy, and I want you to be happy in life. Whether that includes me or not."

She surprised herself by those last words. Something also lifted in her. She meant them. She wanted Billy to have every happiness he deserved. Even if it included walking away from her.

"God will show us the way," she murmured. Whether it's what we want or not, she added to herself.

"He always does," Billy said. He turned toward the back of the wagon and withdrew a burlap bag and an axe. Something had closed off in him. He was shielding part of himself from her. She could feel it.

He clearly was finished talking about their relationship.

"Let's go find that tree," he said.

The novel fun of the outing had faded for Clara.

"I best wait here," she said. "I know I won't have enough breath to trudge uphill and through deep sand at the same time." Let him truly understand her limitations. He had to.

For the first time, Billy looked at her as though realizing he couldn't fix her health, couldn't make his forward path unfold as it had always done, steady and according to his will.

He rubbed a hand across the back of his neck, then smiled at her. "I'll find us a good tree," he said, and started walking uphill.

She watched until he was lost to her sight in a thicket of trees. She wondered if Billy realized he'd said he'd find the two of *them* a good tree, not *you* or *me*. Shouts and laughter echoed from all around her. She scrambled back into the wagon seat and hugged herself. And prayed as though her life depended on it.

On Christmas Eve, Clara gazed at the decorated tree in the parlor and straightened one of the tiny pine-straw basket ornaments. Billy had been right. The bright green scrub pine was sturdy. Its branches supported the decorations despite the thinness of each pine needle.

She started to compare the short, scrubby pine with the tall fir trees of her past Christmases. Just as quickly, she shifted the thought. She'd come to like the smell of pine a great deal. The tree fit into a corner of the room as though grown for the spot. She was glad her family followed the Old World tradition of decorating the tree on Christmas Eve. It made the day even more special. She couldn't wait to look at the decorated tree later that night. The gold and silver paper ornaments would glow in light reflected from the fireplace after they came home from church and built up the fire.

The parlor clock chimed ten times. Clara fixed the shepherd in the crib set so he was positioned in perfect symmetry with the others. Then she hurried upstairs to get ready for Midnight Mass.

PART V

December 25, 1898

Christmas Day and Christmastide

Shared warmth and joy cascaded through the full church and the choir voices echoed off the walls. Midnight Mass was a solemn yet happy celebration and it suffused Clara's soul. She saw peace reflected in the faces of others as they filed out afterwards and bid each other Merry Christmas.

People lingered outside church and chatted in the light of the nearly full moon. Clara saw Billy lope over toward her. He had a jaunt in his step and a smile that melted her heart. And also made it beat faster. He grinned at her and gave an almost imperceptible nod toward her mother, who stood next to her.

As if by some prearranged signal, her mother called out to Meg, who was nearby with Harvey and the rest of the DeForests. Gertrude moved away from Clara and toward the larger group at the same minute Billy reached her.

"Clara, can I talk to you for a minute?" he asked.

She looked from him to her family, who all drifted slightly farther away to greet the Taylor Grove clan. She realized no one was standing near the two of them. That was odd.

"Yes, of course," she said, and responded to his smile with a joy that filled her heart. "You know I like spending time with you. I can't help it."

"Ah, that's good," he said, and placed a hand on her elbow and started to steer her to the back edge of the building, even farther away from congregants and visitors exchanging Christmas greetings near the front door.

He stopped and released her arm.

"Billy, is everything okay?" Clara asked.

He seemed nervous, so unlike him. He leaned against the building, then straightened, then shifted from foot to foot, then leaned against the building again. He alternately crossed his arms over his chest and clasped them behind his back.

"Has something happened?!" She was starting to worry.

"No. Yes."

He halted and drew in a breath. Then reached into the pocket of his suit jacket and withdrew a small box.

Clara's breath skipped in both pleasure and dismay. Was that what she thought it was?

Billy watched her as if trying to read behind her expression.

He swallowed again, cleared his throat and opened the box. Inside lay an exquisite opal ring. Clara's eyes widened.

"It's beautiful," she said.

"It was my mother's. It's for you."

She stared, at a loss for words.

"If you want it, I mean," Billy rushed to get out his next sentences. "Look, uh, I know what we talked about and stuff but it doesn't matter to me. I love you, Clara."

He exhaled as though he'd been holding his breath for long minutes.

"I'd like to give you this ring as a Christmas gift and as a promise for the future," he said.

She started to take a few steps back.

"Wait, I don't mean to scare you, Clara."

She wasn't scared. Emotions of every other kind assaulted her. She wanted to laugh, to cry, to shout yes and throw her arms around Billy, and to yell out no, he couldn't possibly want a life with someone who didn't have everything to give.

A part of her noticed he'd been unable to speak the reality of her situation. He'd said, "what we talked about, and stuff," as though the realities didn't loom as large as she knew they did.

"I'm not scared, Billy," she said, after wrestling her jumbled feelings into a modicum of order. "I'm honored. I'm touched beyond what I can even explain."

"Then why aren't you smiling?" he asked. He no longer looked or acted nervous. Nor did he exude the bright hope he'd approached her with. His shoulders slumped a bit.

"Because I can't accept the ring," she whispered.

He looked at her, smile replaced by an expression of someone trying but failing to understand.

"Why not? You don't care enough for me?"

"Oh, Billy no!" How could she make him understand?

"I'm falling… no, I am in love with you, Billy, and that's exactly why I can't accept the ring—or make the promise."

He waited. She knew she had to say more.

"What we talked about affects the future we'd pledge with this ring," she said.

"I know, Clara. It's okay."

She looked down at the ring he still held out toward her and felt a deep sadness.

"I don't want you to make a promise you might later regret," she said. She held up a hand to stop the protest she saw forming on his lips.

"My shortcomings weigh hard on me," she continued. "I

can't bear to face a future when those realities really hit home for you, for us."

"Clara, you're telling me what you feel, and I appreciate that," Billy said. "But I have feelings too. It's almost like this is all about you."

"What? No!" She pursed her lips and blew out a breath. "It's about both of us."

"That's not what I see or hear. I see someone second-guessing how I'll react down the road," he said.

Clara felt a spark of annoyance. "Maybe I am thinking for both of us," she said. "Because you're not. Thinking ahead, I mean. Like when you were all set to buy that car. You weren't thinking far enough ahead."

They stared at each other for a long minute.

"I wish with all my heart I could say yes," she whispered. "But I can't."

Billy slid the ring box back into his pocket.

"I understand, Clara."

But she knew he didn't.

Clara felt as heavy as the clanking train as it slowed around a curve. She looked out the window of her berth but couldn't make out anything except the shadows of trees, the brilliance of stars in the inky sky, and an occasional puff of smoke from the steam engines.

Next to her, Aunt Hattie snored softly. Her energetic aunt had finally run out of steam. Clara half-smiled in the dark. Run out of steam. Her little pun would be funny if only she didn't feel so depleted herself.

She should be excited. She was finally returning home. She'd see friends and neighbors and bask in the glow of the winter wedding. She'd clung to the dream of this trip for months. Now her enthusiasm was receding the farther they traveled from home. Oh! She'd just thought of Persimmon Hollow as home. She rubbed her temples.

Clara readjusted herself in the small quarters. Sleep eluded her. She'd nodded off on the first leg of the journey. Eaten too much at dinner. Drank overly strong coffee during the delay between train transfers in Jacksonville. The coffee, the heavy food, and the nap combined to keep her awake now.

She fidgeted again and stared out at the sky. Yes, those things were keeping her awake. Not the image of Billy's expression when she'd declined his Christmas gift. Not the sadness in his eyes when she tried to explain why she couldn't accept the beautiful ring—or the promise it represented.

She'd tried to tell him he didn't know what he was doing. She'd said he hadn't thought everything through. He had, he insisted. But she'd come to know Billy quite a bit over the past month. He sometimes spoke before considering his words. Jumped into an endeavor before making sure the plans in his head would emerge into a workable blueprint.

What else could she have done? She was trying to save him from himself. At least that's what she told herself.

A tear trickled out of her eye. She dashed it away. She wouldn't let Billy or her own confusion ruin this trip.

But the heaviness had weighed on her all Christmas Day. She'd seen the mixed pity and compassion and love in her family's eyes. Learned they'd known about the ring because Billy had spoken to her parents beforehand to seek their blessing. They'd spent the day treating her as though she were made of glass and liable to shatter at any moment. That made her even more dejected and more focused on starting her journey the following day.

The season of hope, her mother had called Advent. Hope wasn't supposed to fade when Advent ended. The coming of the

Christ child awakened joy and brought light to the world. Yet right now Clara felt a gloomy sadness.

Was she missing something? Late Christmas night, after everyone else was asleep, Clara had crept into the nook off the living room and prayed before the small home altar her mother had set up there. She stayed for a long time on the kneeler before the crucifix that stood between icons of Christ Pantocrator and of Mary holding the baby Jesus. She'd lit the votive candle while she prayed. The gentle flickering light behind the red glass helped her focus on the calming presence of God.

She didn't find the total peace she craved, but she'd understood she wasn't alone. Christ carried her cross with her. If only he hadn't made it so heavy, she couldn't help but think. Even asked why during one prayer. Then chided herself.

"Jesus, I trust in you. Come, Holy Spirit, please help me," she'd whispered, before blowing out the candle and heading to bed for a few restless hours of sleep.

Now, here she was, awake again. She'd have dark circles under her eyes for the wedding if she didn't get some sleep. She started to say a rosary. "Mary, please ask Jesus to come to my aid," she murmured after she was finished. "I need all the help I can get."

After changing trains again in New York, Clara and Hattie finally arrived in their hometown and hired a carriage to carry them to Hattie's house.

"I can feel this weather in my bones already," Hattie said as the driver stopped in front of her house. "And this damp, cold house won't help until it heats up."

"Anything's better than standing out here," said Clara after she stepped out of the carriage. A mix of icy rain and snow fell in pellets that stung any skin unlucky enough to be exposed to the elements. She pulled her wool cape closer around her and tightened the hood ribbons. The streets were a jumble of slippery snow. The downtown buildings that surrounded the train station had seemed squashed together, giving nothing room to breathe. Even Hattie's quieter neighborhood—her old neighborhood, too —didn't appear as welcoming as in the past. Everything was shadowed and muffled.

"You want to move back here why?" asked Hattie as they trudged up the front walk, followed by the driver and his assistant with their luggage.

Clara was beginning to wonder herself. Her toes chilled as slush seeped in around the shoelace rivets in her boots. Within minutes, her toes were numb. She bowed her head to prevent the sharp wind from reaching her face.

She made it to the porch and sank into a cold rocking chair while Hattie fumbled for her house keys in her large canvas bag. Everything was chilly and dreary and nothing at all like she remembered. The afternoon light had faded quickly and the streets looked gray and gritty in dusk's shadows.

She hoped tomorrow would be brighter.

"I better call Beth and let her know I've arrived," Clara said. "And find out what time the wedding rehearsal is tomorrow." But she made no move to rise from the chair. She was bone weary.

Her aunt unlocked the door and hustled both of them inside.

"You'd better decide what you want from life," Hattie said as they discarded their wet outerwear. "If you ask me, you're throwing away a bright future with that young man back in Florida in exchange for a humdrum life here."

"I didn't ask you," muttered Clara to herself.

"I know what it's like to have life interfere with a nicely mapped-out plan," Hattie said, her brisk tone somewhat softer. "I went from being a wife and mother to a childless widow."

Clara winced. She never thought about Hattie as she must

have been when younger. Or what she must have suffered. Clara had only been nine when the tragedy occurred.

"You break or you get stronger, Clara dear," her aunt continued. "We each forge a different path, sometimes of our own choosing, sometimes not. Don't be afraid to take a step forward, even if you're not sure what the outcome will be. Now, come, let's get a fire going and get warm while the coal stove heats up. The temperature outdoors is dropping by the minute. Dear Lord, get me back to the sunny South, soon!"

Clara found herself almost agreeing. Her toes and fingers had stiffened in the cold. How quickly she'd gotten accustomed to Florida's warmth, she thought, as she helped stack kindling in the fireplace.

The next day, the sun had re-emerged and the rainy snow had stopped. The cold, however, remained. Clara tried to not care. But the freezing air bit into her. She huddled in her cloak as she walked the two blocks to Beth's house.

Once there and warmly welcomed, she threw herself into wedding rehearsals. She was invigorated by the renewed friendships and the festive atmosphere of the upcoming New Year's Eve wedding. The tall, decorated Christmas tree, a blue-green fir, touched the ceiling in the parlor. Its blue and silver theme was echoed in garlands that wrapped the banister all the way up the staircase from which the bride would descend.

Clara stopped mid-step when she saw fern woven into the garland. She needed to tell Billy! He was right, there was a market for ferns in home decorations. A pang rippled through her. The first person she'd thought to tell about her discovery was Billy. The man she'd pushed away.

Clara focused on the rehearsal. She and the other three bridesmaids waited at the bottom of the stairs and joined the procession into the parlor. A set of pocket doors had been opened to the adjacent library and made the room appear double in size.

She had never attended a wedding in a house instead of a

church, but her friend's faith allowed such. The wedding party practiced their steps from the staircase, through the foyer, into the living room and up to the fireplace.

There was just enough space to move between the extra chairs that had been brought in. Glass jars filled with holiday orbs added sparkle to tabletops that would soon be draped in white linen and decorated with blue and white flower arrangements. Arrangements accented by fern.

The house was already filled with relatives and friends and abuzz with motion, talk, and activity. After the rehearsal, Clara and her friends were ushered into the solarium for a light lunch. She sank into a cushioned chair with relief.

The day's excitement was infectious but she felt herself nearing her limit of exertion. They'd practiced the procession three times, she'd been chatting with her friends since the moment she'd arrived, and had been up and down the stairs to try on her bridesmaid gown, admire the wedding gown, and look at everything in the trousseau.

She was glad to be seated. But surprised at the bleakness of the bare tree limbs and winter-shrouded landscape outside the windows that lined the solarium's back wall. She wanted—craved—the bright sunlight and healthy greenery that surrounded her Florida home. Surprised at her reaction, she dug her spoon into a fruit cup with more force than necessary.

"Tell us about Florida, Clara," the bride-to-be asked as the group nibbled on tea sandwiches and fruit. "Do you have a beau down there?" The others chimed in. "Yes, tell us! We want to know everything!" They started talking among and over each other as Clara gathered her thoughts.

Tell them about Billy? How could she explain? She realized she could. These friends would understand her hesitation. They'd been friends since they were toddlers. They knew her and accepted her as she was.

The next thought came as though she'd been thunderstruck.

Yes, Clara, they accept you as you are. Just as Billy accepts you. Wants you as you are. Her eyes widened. The truth was undeniable. Why had she been so obtuse?

She looked around the room, at the house she knew as well as her own, at the faces of dear friends. They were warmly familiar yet somehow unfamiliar. It was as though time and distance had already started molding her into a different person. She shivered. Is that actually what she was afraid of? Afraid to leave safe, familiar childhood and young adulthood and grow into full womanhood in her own individual way?

Did she push Billy away from fear that stemmed not only from her bodily limitations but also because she was afraid to take the next step? As Aunt Hattie had said just yesterday?

"We're waiting, Clara!" sang out the girl seated next to her.

She looked at her dear, dear friends, set down her spoon and inhaled a breath.

"Actually, yes, there is someone," she said, to a flurry of *oohs* and requests for details. "If he's still there when I return."

The wedding was as beautiful as Clara had imagined it would be. A day she'd long remember. She floated back to Aunt Hattie's exhausted but happy after it was over, and with a settled feeling that had eluded her for so long. She'd enjoyed herself, but was ready to return home. And that home was in Persimmon Hollow.

She shared every wedding detail with Hattie, who had spent the day packing and was only mildly interested. But her aunt perked up when Clara explained she no longer wanted to seek new living arrangements.

"I don't know how to explain it, but this city doesn't feel like home any longer," Clara said. "I realized that somewhere between the start of rehearsals and the end of wedding festivities."

"Praise the Lord," Hattie said. "Now get some rest and then help me sort through dishes and clothing, please."

They spent the evening preparing for their return trip and fell asleep before the New Year arrived.

The next morning, despite still being tired, Clara went with Hattie to pay New Year's Day calls. The houses they visited felt overheated and the outdoor winds sharp. Longtime acquaintances no longer felt as close to Clara as they once had.

"Glad that's done," Hattie said as they returned to her house. They used their remaining time to finish packing and get ready for their upcoming departure.

The final morning, Clara and her aunt, accompanied by as many trunks, hatboxes, and suitcases that Hattie could fit on the transport wagon, waited at the station for the train that would carry them back to Florida.

Clara's head was crammed with memories, advice, laughter, whispered drama, a lot of cheer, and a flurry of promises to write and stay friends forever. The wedding had been lovely and she'd been awash in both laughter and tears when everyone waved off the bride and groom. The newlyweds would soon be off on their own adventure, she knew, as homesteaders in the young state of Wyoming.

How quickly all their lives were diverging. She thought about the other bridesmaids. One was happily married to a local businessman and had confided that she was expecting, although not showing yet. A second bridesmaid was recently engaged and the third had just accepted a job as a teacher in the Alaska Territory. Some of her relatives had settled there and opened a mercantile when the population mushroomed with the gold rush.

The museum project she'd left in their care had stalled. None of the others had been able to devote time to it. Each claimed they weren't suited for such an endeavor. They'd returned the planning documents with suggestions she'd heard before.

"Put your skills to use in Florida," they urged. "Surely that state must be in need of culture!"

"You don't know how much," she replied, and took the paperwork and packed it neatly in her luggage.

The train whistle startled her out of her reverie. She looked up at the locomotive lumbering into the station in a belch of smoke. She peered down the track to find the Pullman cars.

"You're smiling," Aunt Hattie said. "Can it be you're actually happy to be returning to Florida?"

"Maybe," said Clara. Then she cast a sidelong glance at her aunt and grinned.

"Hmph," said her aunt. "You can't fool me. You're happier than you're letting on."

"I've accepted that everything has changed—permanently—in just months, Aunt Hattie," Clara said. "I mean, I know life always changes. I just wasn't ready. I wanted to keep it locked into one shape."

"You're ready now?"

"You could say that. I'm still a bit shaky about so much newness in Florida, though."

"That's okay, Clara. Even the most confident person feels apprehensive when their world shifts. The important thing is to accept situations you can't alter. Oh, you fix what you can. As for everything else, you accept and move forward or resist and be miserable."

"I'll be miserable if I don't get out of this smoke," Clara said, as the train screeched to a stop. They rose as a porter escorted them to their rail car.

As the train pulled out, Clara felt lighter than she had in a long time. She might be physically limited, but she was strong. She could face anything.

~

The house was dark and quiet when Melvin and Harvey pulled the wagon up to the DeForest house late the next night. Clara was stiff all over.

"I thought the broken wheel would never get fixed on that train," she said, again, as her brother helped her and Hattie out of the wagon. Harvey started to grab luggage.

"Must have been a tough repair, the train was five hours late getting in," Melvin said. He yawned and stretched. "That's okay, Harvey and I both got some much-needed sleep. The store has been nonstop busy and we spend almost every spare minute working on Harvey and Meg's new house. Harvey is even thinking of starting a construction business. More and more people are moving to town." Before Clara could answer, Melvin had started helping Harvey transfer the rest of the bags.

The men piled the luggage just inside the front door. Harvey waved and headed off to his semi-finished house, where he'd fashioned temporary bachelor's living quarters. The others whispered good nights to one another. Melvin bounded up the stairs and a slow-stepping Hattie almost sleepwalked behind him.

Clara suppressed an urge to laugh. This was the second time in days she'd seen her aunt too tired to talk. Everything really was changing.

Alone, she took her time climbing the stairs. She inhaled the fragrant air, perfumed with the scent of flowering tea olives from sprigs her mother or sister had cut and placed in a vase. She felt joyful and, yes, happy to be home.

She quietly opened the door to the bedroom she shared with Meg. Waning moonlight spilled through the window and across her bed. Clara stopped in mid-step as she gazed at her bed. It was covered with gifts.

She gaped at the array and sank down on the bed in an open spot. No one in the DeForest family received more than a few gifts at Christmas. Everyone got one or two utility items like sleepwear or shoes, and one fancy gift such as a leather-covered journal or silk embroidery floss.

They had exchanged their gifts Christmas morning, the day before she left. Yet her bed was piled with an assortment of packages that didn't appear to have anything to do with utility. The largest didn't even fit on the bed. Pushed up against the bed was a small lemon tree in a large pot. The tree had one ripening fruit on it and a handful of citrus blossoms. Their rich scent sweetened the room.

In the dim moonglow, Clara saw something paper-like dangle from a branch. She untied it and took a closer look. It was a piece of paper cut in the shape of a bird, with the words Day One penciled on it.

Something rustled near her. Clara glanced toward the sound, stood up, squinted and saw the shape of a bird cage emerge from the shadows atop her dresser. Inside, two mourning doves cooed at her. Attached to the cage was another paper bird, with the words Day Two written on it.

A bird in a tree. Two doves. What would she find next? Three hens? Clara's heart began to beat a little faster as she sat back down and started to sort through the remaining gifts. She found a delicate bird's nest made from pine needles. In it rested a tea towel embroidered with three hens along the edge. Another paper bird was pinned to the towel. This bird was labeled with the words Day Three (Real Ones Outside!).

Billy. This had to be Billy's doing. Nobody else would have thought of it.

Excitedly, Clara started a careful sorting of the gifts. A piece of paper labeled Day Four dangled from a ribbon tied around a terrarium globe set atop a thick round piece of cedar wood. She inhaled the clean woodsy scent. Underneath the globe four small wooden birds nestled in—oh, goodness—real mistletoe. A note jotted on the reverse side of the paper said that each bird was calling Clara. She giggled under her breath.

A gift labeled Day Five was a small wooden box. Inside were five golden-looking rings, each handwoven from what had to be Billy's blond hair. She picked up each one and looked at the superb craftsmanship of each intricately woven piece. She wondered who helped Billy with the rings. She doubted the man who didn't know one thread from the next would have a strand of knowledge about the popular art of hair weaving.

The Day Six gift was a duck decoy. Clara frowned. A duck decoy? Beautifully made, but... She untied the paper note labeled both Day Six and Seven. On the other side was a scribbled note: "Sorry, too late to carve six geese or seven swans! Running out of time!"

She smiled and leaned forward to set the decoy on the floor. The bed squeaked. At the same time the doves cooed again, more loudly than before.

"Oh, Clara, good, you're home," Meg mumbled from her bed across the room. "Billy told me those birds need to be set free," she continued, sounding only slightly more awake. "He just wanted you to see them. You know, so you'd have the full effect of the Twelve Days of Christmas."

Meg bolted upright in bed. "Good gosh, Clara! You don't know yet!"

"I do now!" Clara said. "What a fabulous surprise." Since Meg was awake, she turned on the electric light on her dresser to chase the shadows. "Only Billy would have thought of this!"

Only Billy would be so clever and generous—after her dismissal of him—to show her in such a unique way that he was ready and waiting. If and hopefully when she was ready. And she was. At least for the first steps.

"No, no, you don't know," Meg said, scrambling out from under her quilt and crossing the room to Clara. She put her arm around Clara. "It's Billy. He's hurt. I mean, really hurt. His leg is broken. Everyone thought it was beyond saving at first. Then a fever set in and infection. He's in bad shape. Really bad shape."

Every hard-won note of optimism drained from Clara. Her legs felt heavy. She sat down hard on the bed and then stood back up. It seemed all her blood pooled in her feet. She became so light-headed she plopped back down on the bed.

"I have to go to him."

"You can't!" Meg said. "Not right now. It's almost two o'clock in the morning. At first daylight, we'll go. I promise."

"Why didn't anybody contact me, telephone or send a telegram?"

"Everything happened so fast," Meg said. "Nobody knew right away he was hurt. He's always out and about and no one worried about his absence. But when he missed dinner the men formed a rescue squad and went looking. It was almost dark by the time they found him. The angle of the break was so bad he'd been unable to even crawl back to his wagon. Almost overnight, fever set in. He started to get delirious."

Clara twisted the folds of her dress and fidgeted with the fabric. The odd realization that she hadn't yet changed out of her winter wool traveling clothes flitted through her mind. The doves cooed again. The journey she'd pinned her escapist hopes on had instead led her back to her true home. Was she to lose the newfound joy of Billy already?

She fumbled for her pocket inside her skirt but her fingers trembled too much. She unhooked her shoes, kicked them off, unhooked the skirt at the waistband and let its heavy weight slide to the floor. She stepped out of it, shedding the northern garb.

She reached again into her hand-embroidered pocket, tied around her waist over her chemise and petticoat, and withdrew her rosary. The faintest scent of roses clung to the beads.

"Pray with me?" she asked Meg, who by now sat next to her.

They bowed their heads. "I believe in God, the Father Almighty…" they began in whispered words.

By the time they'd recited the Sorrowful Mysteries and said

the last Amen after the Hail Holy Queen, Clara felt calmer and closer to peace.

"Billy is in your hands, God," she murmured. "Thy will be done, I know." She set down the rosary and gripped her hands together. "But please, would you make that what I want, too."

Their mother tapped on the half-open bedroom door and walked in. "I heard you praying," she said as she re-tied the belt on her robe. "Clara, we're all praying for Billy's recovery." She hugged her daughter and kissed the top of her head.

Clara clung to her. "Is it wrong to want God's will to be exactly what I want? I need to let Billy know how much I've thought about things, how much I care for him—love him, I think. No, I know. I do love him. Mama, he can't die!"

Gertrude and Meg both encircled Clara and held her close. The doves cooed.

"We all ask God to grant wishes," Gertrude said. "The hard part sometimes is accepting the answer he delivers. Everything will look brighter in the morning. We're in a joyous season of light. We waited with hope for the arrival of Jesus and now he shines on us with his presence. Keep that hope alive in your heart, Clara. But try—for your own health—to get some sleep."

Clara lay awake long after her mother left the room and Meg fell back asleep. She'd battled health issues since babyhood and look at her. She never felt stronger. Billy was stronger yet, and tougher. He'd come through. She knew it. She hoped it.

She tossed and turned and finally fell asleep reciting the ancient Jesus prayer: "Lord Jesus Christ, have mercy on me."

PART VI

January 5, 1899

Epiphany

Daylight arrived on Epiphany Eve in a mix of gentle colors. Clara was up and dressed before her mother or anyone else stoked the fire in the stove. She added kindling, prepared coffee in the percolator pot, and set the pot on the stove.

The smell of coffee soon drew the rest of the family to the kitchen.

"Clara, leaving already?" her mother asked as she glanced at her fully dressed daughter. "Let your brother eat first and hitch the wagon for you."

"I'll walk to Taylor Grove if I have to," Clara said.

Melvin came bounding down the stairs as they spoke. "Hold on, sis, I'll have you set in a jiffy."

"I'll go, too, and make sure she doesn't over-exert herself, Mother," Meg said as Clara fidgeted and paced.

Without waiting for breakfast, Clara and Meg set out for Taylor Grove as soon as Melvin pulled the wagon around.

"I'm beginning to understand Billy's excitement about that Winton car," Clara said as they made their slow way across the two miles that separated Taylor Grove from the heart of town. "He said it could reach speeds of thirty miles per hour. We'd be at the grove already."

She scrambled out of the wagon almost before Meg halted the horse at the Taylors' large log cabin.

The inside front door opened before she reached the top step onto the porch.

"He's out of danger! The fever broke!" Polly called as she opened the screen door for them.

Clara sagged against the door frame in relief.

"He'll mend even faster when he sees you," Polly said, and pulled her inside, with Meg right behind.

"Hey is that Clara I hear?" a weak voice called from farther inside the house.

"Billy!" Clara cried out. "Yes, yes, it's me! Oh, Billy, it's so good to hear you. I missed you so much." She started toward the sound of his voice, which seemed to be coming from the kitchen. Polly put a hand out to halt her.

"Be prepared," she said. "He's in rough shape."

Polly and Meg trailed after her as she almost ran into the kitchen. Clara came to such a quick halt when she entered the room they bumped into her from behind.

A pale Billy lay atop a bed that had been moved near the stove for warmth. A cast encased his leg from foot to mid-thigh. The leg was propped up atop a thick cushion of several folded quilts. His face and arms bore scratches from tree branches and a puffy lump protruded from his forehead.

He started to shift upward in bed. Clara recoiled from the pain that crossed his face.

"Don't you dare move," she said in a half-scolding, half-tender voice. She knelt down beside the bed and laid a hand on his forehead, careful to avoid the lump. He still felt a bit feverish.

"I wish I could hug you," she said. "Kiss you. Be close to you forever. Be wrapped in your arms." She moved her hand to cover one of his.

"You mean that?"

"Billy Taylor, you think I'd have said it otherwise? You best hurry and recover and you'll see how much I mean it. I plan to start with twelve kisses, one for each of the Twelve Days of Christmas. Oh, Billy, I so loved your surprise gifts. Thank you."

The old Billy grin appeared for the first time and he responded with a weak chuckle. "Thought you'd like it. Good, so good, to see you, Clara. Glad you're back."

He left the next question in his eyes as he looked at her.

"I'm back in a lot of ways," she said. "All ways, if you know what I mean."

His hand squeezed hers in a light grip. Their gazes met. Yes, he knew. She saw how much.

Clara leaned in and placed a whisper of a kiss on his lips. "Rest now and get your strength back. I'll come see you every day." She stood up. As she turned around she saw the entire Taylor and Gomez families hovering behind her. All seemed very interested in the conversation. Meg stood off a little to the side. Her happiness for Clara filled her face.

Clara didn't care if her courtship was playing out in public, out in the open, in a large family kitchen in front of everyone. She felt she been apart from Billy for months instead of days. She didn't want to leave him again.

Slow, steady breathing signaled that Billy was dozing.

Polly let out a long breath. "It was good to hear Billy cheer come back into his voice," she said. "Even I was afraid I'd never hear it again, and I don't scare easily. Thank you, Clara."

"No, thank God for waking me up," Clara said. "Thank God for not taking Billy away from me."

"This was the first time he smiled since he took that stupid fall," Polly said.

"How did it happen?" Clara asked. "I only know the general details."

"It was right after you left," Polly said. "He climbed a tree out by the river to harvest mistletoe for one of your Twelve Days gifts. He'd been working on them for a while by then and had several finished. Mistletoe was still on his list. He slipped while high in the tree and fell. He was too far from anywhere to get help. He said he yelled until he was hoarse and then passed out from the pain. The doctor came as soon as we got him home and just in time, too, to save his leg but he said it'd be touch and go for a few days. Between the pain and the shock, Billy was agitated. Made me promise to finish the mistletoe gift and cart the completed ones to your house. Meg helped me. Then the fever set in."

Clara took a step back as Polly's words sunk in. "He could have died."

"I'm not that easy to get rid of." Billy was awake again.

Clara smiled when she heard the familiar Billy in the tone of his comment. "Nobody's happier about that than I am," she said.

"Are you sure you're the same doubt-filled Clara who left us less than two weeks ago?" Polly asked.

"Yes, I am. Only this Clara has come to her senses about the love of a good man I'd be lost without." She spoke without looking at Polly. She stared directly at Billy.

"I'm not dreaming?" Billy asked, with a grin that belied the question. "You know, I feel better already. I think I'll get up."

Clara, Meg, and every other adult in the room stepped forward with hands outstretched and orders to stay put.

Meg turned toward Clara. "We better leave for a while, Clara, or they'll never get him to rest."

"No—" Billy started to say.

"Yes," Clara finished whatever he was going to say. "You'll rest better without distractions. Besides, I've got to get back home. I have some hens to take care of." She waited for a chuckle and was gratified when she heard it.

"Doves, too," she added. "But," she swallowed before she spoke again and mustered her courage. She normally shrank from public displays of deeply personal feelings.

"Just know that I love you," she whispered.

Silence. Had she said the wrong thing?

Billy reached, took her hand and squeezed it while he locked gazes with her.

"Clara, I love you, too."

Clara felt as bright and light as the day, filled with every hope and happiness of the season. "I'll visit every day. We have so much to do!"

"Can't wait to begin," he said. "Wait for me."

"Forever," she said.

At Epiphany Mass on January 6, the joy of the Magi story and its reminder of Christ's arrival in the world cast blessings of new beginnings into Clara's heart. Gone were the stubbornness, the resistance to accept help, and the refusal to step into change. She truly understood, maybe for the first time, how Advent—the season of hope—leads to light that fills the soul.

PART VII

EPILOGUE

June, 1899

Clara sat at a long table in the auditorium of DeLand Academy and College. She hummed as she pondered ideas for potential displays of the items neatly laid across every inch of the table. Everything from ancient artifacts to botanical specimens to fairly recent settlement implements set aside for future posterity was arranged before her. She never imagined she'd care about such things. But each piece was a tiny window to this place she'd come to call home.

They all were part of a new museum being established at the college. It was a dream of a project. After learning of her previous museum-organizing experience, the Academy principal, Eunice Alloway Williams, and College archaeology professor Nate Russo asked her to help organize and catalogue the college's collection. They also requested that she devise themed exhibit ideas. She was delighted.

Read the story of Nate and his love, Penelope, in Growing A Family in Persimmon Hollow (Persimmon Hollow Legacy, Book 3)

Billy sat reading nearby, his long legs fully healed and stretched up and feet resting on a windowsill. Sunshine poured into the room from the large windows that lined the walls.

"Found it," he said, and placed his feet back on the floor and sat up. He grabbed a piece of Clara's notepaper and started jotting down numbers from the volume in his lap.

"These two formulas will allow me to do side-by-side fertilizer tests to see which one is better for the ferns. This first one is almost the same as what Lue and I devised, but testing is the only way to find out for sure if it's the best one."

He slid the note in his pocket and set down the book. He stood, moved behind Clara, placed his hands on her shoulders and leaned down to kiss her cheek and the back of her neck.

She set down her pen and reached up to wrap her hands over his. She leaned back, closed her eyes and murmured a slight "Mmm" as she tilted her head back.

Billy's lips found hers.

Neither heard the footsteps.

"Hey, you're not married yet," called Polly from the doorway. She hesitated for a moment and then marched in. "You done with that book? I need it for my class. I'm giving a surprise quiz today."

Billy straightened and gave Polly a fake scowl but kept one hand on Clara's shoulder. Clara giggled and kept her hand tucked into his.

"Six more months," said Billy. "Can't wait. I'm counting the days until I can carry this beautiful woman across the threshold."

Both he and Polly looked at Clara, who felt a blush start to creep up her neck.

"I can't wait either," Clara whispered, but still felt shy about saying such words aloud in public. Her lifelong reticence and withdrawn behavior had protected her for so long. She'd hidden behind propriety, but she now realized she'd used it partly as a screen. Her inner being hadn't changed, but her joy and acceptance of life had.

Clara was still amazed at how much life and people in Persimmon Hollow had thawed her defenses with their open, loving, and honest ways. And how a small town offered its own special opportunities. Different from those of a city, perhaps, but intriguing for those who looked.

Clara voiced her gratitude to God each night during evening prayers. That was another thing about Persimmon Hollow. She couldn't quite put her finger on it. She felt closer to God here. She'd become more invested in her faith and she appreciated the closeness of the Catholic community.

And Billy. Always Billy. She knew he'd put his life on the line to protect her. He was eagle-eyed about her health. He'd set out to learn as much about her condition as he did about agriculture. Instead of being an obstacle in their relationship, her physical fragilities were simply a part of her that they navigated together. She was able to relax and stop worrying about the future.

Even her family had stopped hovering so much and overly protecting her movements after they saw how Billy walked the journey with her.

A thunder of smaller footsteps rumbled up the stairs and down the hall to the room.

"Miss Clara!" called little Fannie Taylor as she halted at the doorway. She waved a letter in her hand and led a pack of her classmates who piled behind her. They pushed inside, laughing and talking over one another.

"You have a letter!" said Fannie. "From the Alaska Territory!" she shouted. "The postmaster from the Mercantile just dropped it off here and said you'd want something so important right away."

The youngsters ran in a clump toward her. Billy gave her shoulder a slight squeeze as she withdrew her hand to accept the letter. She thanked the youngsters. They chorused, "you're welcome." But they didn't leave. Just stood there, clustered around her with expectant, hopeful looks.

"Are you gonna read it?" a little boy asked.

"Apparently, right now," she said, but her lips edged up into a smile.

She scanned the handwriting and saw small hands on the arms of her chair as the shorter pupils leaned in. She felt breath over her shoulder from the taller ones.

"It's from my friend who's a teacher in the Alaska Territory," she said.

She heard "wow" and "where's that?"

"If your teacher approves, I'll come to your class and read the letter to you and we can talk about Alaska. It's quite a wilderness up there."

The group thundered out of the room as one. Their calls for their teacher echoed along with their footsteps.

"Maybe pupils in other classes would also like to hear about Alaska," she said to Billy and Polly. "And out at the orphanage and the neighborhood school."

"I know they all would," Polly said. "I'll arrange it."

Billy took Clara's hands and helped her rise, only to fold her in his arms. She wrapped her arms around him and rested her head on his chest. Polly quietly slipped out of the room.

"I know a double wedding with your sister and Harvey at Christmas is the big plan, and I know it'll be swell, but, geez, Miss DeForest, you make it awfully tough for a guy to wait to call you Mrs. Taylor."

She raised her head and grinned as their gazes met.

"The time will go fast, I promise," she said. "Besides, you need to grow a lot of ferns for decorations."

He guffawed. "Nice try. I've got enough now. Speaking of which," he stopped, stepped back a few steps and withdrew a watch fob from his pocket. "Look at the time! I gotta get out to the fernery, then back to the grove to help Dad. See how you distract me?"

"You love every minute of it," she teased.

He gave her the boyish grin that melted her. "You're right."

He leaned in and kissed her again. "Love you," he said.

"I love you, Billy Taylor," she said, and relished each word.

She sat back in her chair as he left, wrapped in happiness. She looked out the window and saw a mockingbird land on a nearby oak branch. It sang a loud, lilting song of joy. Clara walked over to the window and leaned out.

"I feel the same way," she said to the bird that basked in the summer day. She'd fully emerged from a wilderness she'd languished in for too long. A wilderness she now understood had been of her own making, and one she'd never get stuck in again.

Would she and Billy have a child? Could she? Maybe. She was content to leave the answer in the hands of God and medical science. Her stamina increased the longer she was in Persimmon Hollow. No, she'd never be as physically strong as others. But she was strong enough. In mind, spirit, and body.

END

AFTERWORD

A Chinese horticulturist named Lue Gim Gong (1857 or 1860-1925) spent most of his life in the United States. He lived and worked in DeLand, Florida, for many years and is buried there. He was an award-winning horticulturist of renown, but he also faced discrimination due to his Chinese ethnicity. To learn more about the real man whose fictional counterpart appears briefly in Circle of Light, A Persimmon Hollow Christmas Novella, see his entry in Wikipedia, in a Rollins College blog entry, and on the website of the Orange County Regional History Center.

ABOUT THE AUTHOR

Gerri Bauer is the author of three Persimmon Hollow novels and two novellas. She also writes short stories, biographies, and other nonfiction, and blogs about life in pioneer Florida. A former journalist, she also worked in university communications.

Learn more at gerribauer.com

ALSO BY GERRI BAUER

At Home in Persimmon Hollow

Persimmon Hollow Legacy Book 1

2015/2022

Stitching A Life in Persimmon Hollow

Persimmon Hollow Legacy Book 2

2016/2022

Growing A Family in Persimmon Hollow

Persimmon Hollow Legacy Book 3

2021/2022

Trust in Love

A Persimmon Hollow Novella

2018

Circle of Light

A Persimmon Hollow Christmas Novella

2023

www.ingramcontent.com/pod-product-compliance
Lightning Source LLC
Chambersburg PA
CBHW020412130626
46549CB00006B/2533